E.D. HACKETT

An Unfinished Story

Story One of the Block Island Saga

Second edition

ISBN: 978-1-7374679-1-5

This book was professionally typeset on Reedsy.
Find out more at reedsy.com

You never know how gentle encouragement can change your life. Thank you L.N. for nudging me toward writing my book.

Thank you K. H. and C.M. for cheering me on the entire way. The constructive feedback has been monumental.

Contents

Acknowledgement

For my entire life, I have used writing to an outlet to deal with life. The very first story I wrote was about how I lost my first tooth. I was in first grade. The book was bound and hand illustrated. Every now and then I look back at that story and think about the little girl who had high hopes of using the written word to change lives. I dreamed of being a famous author, writing from my cottage overlooking the wild Atlantic in Ireland.

I kept a journal from the age of ten all the way up until motherhood. I wrote journals specifically to my children from the day I found out I was pregnant until the day they were born. I was afraid that if I died in childbirth, they wouldn't know who I was. Those journals, dedicated to them, contained my soul.

I have always been a reader, using books to escape from the boredom and experiences of my childhood. I still read the last chapter before I start a book, in fear that I will die before I can finish.

Ever since I was a child, my desired superpower was to live other people's lives. I believed that the only way to fully understand others was to walk in their shoes, and what better way than to live their lives. Writing books was my answer to fulfilling my superpower.

This novel may never have happened without the encouragement to just do it. After many years of dreaming about being an author but not actually pursuing it, I jumped off that ledge and wrote. I had no idea what I was doing and probably did most things inefficiently, but I got it done with moments of frustration and self-doubt, but also joy and excitement.

Hitting that publish button filled me with pure joy. I finally did it. I could confidently call myself an author, or a writer, or a novelist.

I couldn't have done it without all the friends and family in my corner who pushed me to take a chance. My husband, Kris, and my mother, Cynthia, have always been my head cheerleaders. No matter what crazy idea I threw at them, they always supported me and problem solved with me when things got tough.

My children, Dylan and Shelby, have watched me grow as a writer. They saw me create a goal and reach it (after many long and agonizing months). I hope one day they look back at all the late nights and early mornings where they watched me write, and recognize that they too can follow their dreams and I will be supporting them every step of the way.

Chapter 1

It was a hot and humid day in Boston. The city bustled with people intermingling in all directions. People rushed to the nearest train station to get to work on time, and others leisurely walked to class. Boston was full of young people, Joanie noticed. Young people who had their entire lives in front of them. A life of making mistakes, learning, growing, and hopefully not falling into the same rut she did.

When she went to college, she thought a business degree would lead her to money, and money would lead her to happiness. Now, she sat in a cubicle eight hours a day managing a team of young reporters for the local newspaper. She knew the minutes were ticking down before newspapers became obsolete.

She had been unhappy at work for years, but the benefits were great, and honestly, what else would she do? Her years of service pigeonholed her into print media, and she didn't feel valued in any other area of commerce. Sure, there were many options within Boston, but who would hire her? She had no fashion sense, didn't wear makeup, and was past her prime for television media. It was just easier to stay put and live a mundane life of cubicles, the sound of typing, and deadlines. At least it was a steady paycheck for now.

Joanie prided herself in her ability to live alone in the expensive metropolitan area. It was almost a badge of honor to prove to those around her that she was successful enough to live the posh life in Boston. No one had to

1

know that her cabinets overflowed with pasta and her freezer overflowed with frozen pizza and ice cream. There was no one there to judge her, so she often sat alone eating dinner in front of the television.

Joanie was never one for people. She found small talk irritating and fatiguing. It was challenging to know what questions to ask or how much information to give about herself. Living alone and not venturing into the city on weekends was much less stressful. Her life felt predictable, safe, and ordinary, and Joanie thought that predictable, safe, and familiar would make her feel content. But, somehow, as she approached her 40th birthday, she felt sad, disappointed, and dissatisfied by how things had unfolded so far.

As Joanie walked into the building, a wave of cool air greeted her, and Joanie shivered in front of the central air vent with gratitude. She gave a quick wave to the building attendant and made her way to the elevator. Joanie had a meeting scheduled with her boss, Mark. Every Monday, they sat down together and talked about the weekend events and topics to target for the following weekend. Joanie organized eight to twelve stories in the Lifestyle section for Sunday's paper.

It was a fun section to assign because it often required her staff to go out and talk to people about what they thought was important. It required research and personal interaction, which helped keep her department upbeat and cheerful. Plus, the topics weren't life-shattering, so writing pieces about the rise of coffee shops and the fall of bookstores wasn't quite as stressful as writing about the latest tornado to hit the Midwest. Joanie's job was to assign the topics to the staff, read and edit their writing, and make sure everything was in by the deadline.

Joanie entered Mark's office and found the entire department crammed around the conference table. Some people stood, some sat, and some wedged themselves in between the filing cabinets. Joanie felt surprised and concerned. Usually, these meetings were for the department heads only. "What's going on?" Joanie asked no one in particular.

The young, blond intern, whose name Joanie couldn't remember, whispered, "Rumor has it that someone might buy the company." The blonde intern chattered away, but Joanie couldn't follow what she was saying. That couldn't be right. Joanie just got a raise. Of course, they wouldn't do that if the newspaper wasn't doing well financially, would they?

The young, bubbly intern spoke about the rumors she heard. Joanie learned that she wanted to change her major first thing tomorrow, and she wasn't going to tell her parents. The group around her started mumbling all at once. The room suddenly went from quiet to raucous. Even though Joanie couldn't read their lips or hear their words, she read their faces, and there was concern among them all.

As a department head, she felt she needed to do something to stop the chaos. Joanie looked around the room and tried to wave her arms and raise her voice above the mumbling and grumbling. Nothing worked. She pressed into the water cooler, which blocked her petite frame from being seen.

The lights flickered three times. Suddenly it was quiet. There was no movement. Everyone turned to the door, and there stood Mark in his short and stocky stature. He couldn't quite make it into the room or squeeze himself in between the conference chairs and wall, so he pulled a chair in from the lobby and stood on the seat. "Attention, everyone!" he bellowed. "I have some news to share." He didn't smile, but his voice carried confidence as if he had been practicing this speech all morning. His brow line furrowed, and purple bags shined under the fluorescent lights. His disheveled clothes looked worn, and Joanie noticed he was wearing one black and one navy blue shoe. His physical presentation did not match the way he delivered his message. Joanie made eye contact and smiled, trying to emit reassurance to whatever message he was sending.

"As you know, the newspaper numbers have been steadily decreasing over the past eight years," Mark started. "Our business manager met with me last week, and we reviewed the finances. Unfortunately, it doesn't look good, and we will be filing bankruptcy. Not just us, but the entire company. People are no longer getting their news through print. Everything is online. We don't have the numbers to support continued print media or any sort of media for that matter. I suppose if we get bought out, we may have the ability to keep some of our jobs through a transfer to the new company, but if bankruptcy goes through, we all will be searching for a new job. I'm sorry. I will be meeting with you individually to discuss your options, but I wanted you all to hear the news at once. So please go back to work and continue your day as planned. You are all dismissed."

As quickly as he appeared, he was gone. Just as before, noise erupted within the tiny conference room. Joanie was surprised but not shocked. She knew this day would come; she just didn't believe it would happen today. Joanie exited the room and slowly walked back to her desk, hiding behind her cubicle. She placed her head in her hands, unable to think.

When she first got this job, she was young and enthusiastic and excited to begin her first internship in college. All she did for those six months was get coffee, order lunch for her supervisor Mikayla, shred paper, and file articles, but she didn't care. Finally, she had her foot in the door, and she was determined to make this the start of something big. She worked hard during college and gave her all to every internship her program threw at her. As she walked the stage at graduation, she knew great things would happen. Confidence and pride overpowered her, and she was ready to take on the world.

After Joanie graduated from college, she applied to every newspaper, magazine, and online journalism outlet she could find within a thirty-mile radius. After six months of rejection, Joanie accepted a job waitressing and bartending to pay the bills. After one excruciating night, she stepped off the subway train, and three young men grabbed her purse and ran.

The very next day, Joanie quit her job. She was broke and scared and needed to do something. She reached out to Mikayla and asked if there was anything open at the paper.

Mikayla didn't respond to Joanie's email for five days and those five days were tough. First, Joanie thought Mikayla was busy and just hadn't gotten around to it, then Joanie thought Mikayla was ignoring her for not keeping in touch more consistently. Then Joanie thought Mikayla had no idea who she was and had deleted her email.

Joanie fretted around her house for days, afraid to go out after dark. She applied to retail jobs and administrative assistant jobs and hid all the incoming mail. Finally, on day five, Joanie heard the familiar ding of her email and sucked in her breath when she saw Mikayla's name in the sender line. She was scared to open it. What if Mikayla had no idea who she was? What if Mikayla had interns that came after her and were more organized, chipper, and hardworking than Joanie? What if Mikayla felt terrible for her for not getting a job sooner? Joanie closed her eyes and clicked the email open.

Hi Joanie! Joanie read in Mikayla's high-pitched, shrill voice. It was so great to hear from you. Sorry it took so long for me to get back to you. I asked around to see if anyone needed additional help in their departments. There is an opening for a part-time Lifestyle reporter if you are interested in applying. It's not a lot of hours, but it is a paid position. You can find the job description link below. Please let me know if you have any questions. Mikayla Moore, Editor.

Joanie slammed down her laptop screen and jumped up and down with excitement. A wide grin plastered across her face, and she forcefully relaxed her lips. Yes, yes, yes! Joanie thought. Finally, an opportunity to get her career on the right path! Part-time? Who cares! A job is a job is a job! Joanie grabbed a fresh cup of coffee, opened her laptop, and started the application process.

Life seemed full of opportunity, possibility, and growth. That was fifteen long years ago.

Chapter 2

"Would you like tea or coffee today?" Carly asked the young couple sitting in her dining room. They were on their honeymoon, enjoying the rocky coastline of Block Island. The waves crashed against the coast as high tide slowly approached the dunes. The sun rose a few hours ago. Every morning Carly woke at 4:30 to watch the sunrise and prepare breakfast for the morning guests.

It was a slower week, and Carly thought it was due to the drop in the number of ferry rides connecting the island to the mainland. Carly had three rooms to clean and care for this weekend. None of the guests had small children, which Carly found relaxing but also immensely quiet. Carly grew up on the island, so sharing her favorite places that most tourists never found kept her guests happy and excited to return.

Carly worked the room with a coffee pot in one hand and a teapot in the other. She loved to ask the guests about their lives back home. What did they do for work? Where did they live? Why did they come to Block Island? Block Island was a tiny island off the coast of Rhode Island near the tip of Long Island. Martha's Vineyard and Nantucket were more well-known than Block Island, so Carly always found it interesting to learn why people chose to come here instead of the others.

"Emma, how has your weekend been so far?" Carly asked the young newlywed sitting at the small table facing the large picture window. Emma smiled up at Carly while cupping the hot teacup in her hand and commented on the beautiful scenery, kind people, and delicious seafood. Carly smiled back. She relied on feedback and reviews to make her bed and breakfast even more desirable. Positive reviews meant more business, which meant more money in her pocket.

She worked her way around the room and chatted noncommittally with a retired couple from New Jersey and a single woman who photographed weddings. Seeing as how it was Sunday, all three rooms were checking out that day. Carly knew she had a busy day cleaning, restocking the fridge, doing laundry, and tending to the garden. Sundays were her favorite day of the week because they allowed her to reflect on her guests' experiences, decompress from the weekend, and brainstorm ways to make the next round of guests' experiences even better.

When the last guest checked out for the day, Carly flopped on the sofa within her private living space. The meteorologist predicted 90 degrees today with a wet, humid feel. Instead of jumping to the dishes, Carly turned on the television, grabbed a cup of tea, and fell into the world of reality television.

Sometimes she wondered what life would have been like if she left the island right out of high school and never returned. All her friends went to college, and Carly left too, but her quickly aging parents put a wrinkle in her plans.

When Carly's parents were in their 40's, the double line on the pregnancy stick was the surprise of their life. They felt too old to bring a child into the world but were devout Catholics and believed it was God's plan all along. When they had a successful business with a predictable routine, two pink lines completely upturned their future. They wanted children when they were younger, but now they felt incapable of caring for a child. Confusion settled between them, unsure how to feel. Was the proper emotion joy, fear, or anger? How would they manage juggling the life of a child and running a business at their age?

When Carly was ten, she noticed the wrinkles that lined her father's forehead and the gray hair covering the top of his head. Carly saw her mother's round middle and relaxed-fit jeans. She noticed the heavy breathing when her dad shoveled snow. In fifth grade, Carly realized her parents were old. Without any siblings, she relied on her girlfriends' mothers to guide her to dress, do her hair, and eventually apply makeup.

Carly's parents lived a life in constant motion and eventually constant fatigue from running the bed and breakfast. It was only a matter of time before it impacted their health. The day before Carly's 30th birthday, her dad, Peter, had a heart attack. He was in the yard mowing the grass, and her mother was at the market restocking on fresh fruit and vegetables. The doctor said it was instant, but Carly often wondered if that was true. Maybe if they lived on the mainland, the proximity to a hospital and good doctors would have saved him.

Carly moved to Maine when she was in her late twenties to the chagrin of her parents. Carly's father passed away the day before her thirtieth birthday. She lived with a lobster fisherman and was happy. She knew that her mom couldn't run the business independently. Without any siblings, Carly felt torn. Her mom barely had time to grieve, what with the busy summer months full of bookings ahead of her. Carly reluctantly returned home. Just for the summer, until her mom got back into the routine. She returned home to help but never left. She let her fisherman slip away.

When Carly was thirty-six, her mom, Ruth, turned seventy-eight. Ruth made an appointment with the local doctor but never made it to him. She had a stroke, which interfered with walking, talking, and feeding herself. Ruth was diagnosed with mild dementia five years prior, so she could no longer care for herself. Carly couldn't take care of her either. Her mom went to the nursing home just a ferry ride away and had been there ever since. That was three and a half years ago.

Carly struggled with whether or not she could go back to Maine and back to the life she adored. She decided to stay on the island and take over the legacy her parents left her, just until Ruth passed away. After that, Carly planned on returning to her old life and hoped it would be an easy transition.

Carly visited Ruth every Wednesday. She transported Ruth's laundry back and forth, brought her gifts and snacks, and tried her best to make the end of her life as best as it could be.

Carly had a choice when her mom got sick. She could convince Ruth to sell the Willowside Inn so she could move back to Maine or take over the business and try to make it work. Her mother would have been devastated if she sold it, so Carly decided the best thing to do was hang onto it until her mother died and then determine her next move. Once Ruth was gone, there was no reason to feel guilty for throwing her family's livelihood away. Carly didn't wish for that day, but she knew that she was approaching forty and probably missed her opportunity to follow her dreams. When this place sold, Carly would be ecstatic to leave the island for good.

Chapter 3

Joanie sat in front of her computer, staring at the home screen. Her fingers were paralyzed, unable to press any keys. Should she look for a new job? New apartment? New roommate? She knew, as of today, she still had a job, but the uncertainty of it, with no savings in place, was giving her a headache. Her family was under the impression that she lived an extraordinary life in a fantastic city with a tremendous career. If she told them that her house of cards was going to crumble at any given moment, shame and embarrassment would wash over her. She would feel like such a failure.

Joanie closed her computer and decided it could wait another day. In the meantime, she would look for a second job to put some money away. Should she find a roommate? That would be a terrible idea, Joanie decided, unless it was necessary. Joanie would rather live in her sister's basement than live with a stranger.

It was Saturday, the day after the big announcement, and the sun was shining. The weatherman forecasted hot weather with less humidity. Joanie wiped her brow, anticipating the heat that would develop over the next few days.

Mark gave her a summer assignment for the Lifestyle section of the paper. Joanie usually delegated article topics to her teammates and didn't understand why Mark gave her this task. He explained that she was one of the most senior employees and deserved some fun. Plus, she didn't have a husband or kids, so there wouldn't be any logistical factors interfering with completing the assignment.

For the next eight weeks, Joanie would document the pros and cons of island living as judged by the community. Joanie had three choices: Martha's Vineyard, Nantucket, or Block Island. All three locations entailed almost a full day of travel. With Joanie being in charge of the Lifestyle section, she knew she needed to either only travel on the weekends or work remotely from the island. Working remotely would be fine as long as the wi-fi was adequate. Her Boston apartment would be empty, which made her nervous.

Joanie had never been to any of those three islands and all the things she read, saw, or heard, screamed money in Joanie's mind. She was nervous to socially engage with people who lived on a different tier of life.

Joanie's daily goal was financial survival, and she imagined that the people who lived there only wanted to have fun, regardless of the cost. She imagined beautiful, bikini-clad women laying on the beach, with a fruity drink in their hands. She saw balconies overlooking the ocean, country clubs, and Jaguars. She wondered if the "vacation" Mark wrapped up in a bow for her would end up being a social nightmare. Joanie needed to connect with these people to write the articles, and she wasn't sure if she had the social etiquette to pull it off credibly. She already felt like an imposter, and she hadn't even decided which island to infiltrate.

She knew that Martha's Vineyard and Nantucket were extremely pricey, and the cost to stay overnight would be high. The newspaper was struggling, so Joanie felt a responsibility to be money-conscious when searching for accommodations. She knew very little about Block Island, but her sister's boyfriend grew up there, so maybe he knew of something or someone who could house her for a few weeks. She made a mental note to give her sister a call.

In the meantime, Joanie reopened her laptop and searched for Block Island, Nantucket, and Martha's Vineyard. She looked at the cost: the ferry ride, accommodations, things to do, and food. This assignment was a Hail Mary to get more people interested in the paper, but Joanie felt it was a death sentence.

Was Mark trying to exhaust all funds before the sale? Was he trying to make the newspaper go bankrupt? Joanie decided that it didn't matter what she thought; she was just following orders. If he wanted to waste the last of the money on a "vacation," then who was she to question it? She would take her assignment seriously, do her best to make the paper proud, and live like a local.

Joanie opened her laptop and continued researching. Seeing as how she was going to be staying overnight, the cost of accommodations was crucial. All three islands presented the same obstacles. The bustling environment in the summer and the isolated setting in the off-season caused Joanie concern. It seemed that fishing, tourism, and old family wealth were the main reasons people stayed year-round.

Joanie decided that the cost of accommodation would be the final factor in where she would crash for the next few months. Seeing how summer already started, it appeared that she wasn't going to be selective in her final arrangement. Joanie joined random groups for all three locations on the internet to ask questions and get leads about apartments. She continued to research, went to the library, and drove to the coast of Rhode Island and the shore of Cape Cod to chat it up with locals who had a different view of life on the islands. Her gut instinct told her that Block Island was the direction to focus her attention on, so Joanie did just that.

* * *

"Welcome to The Willowside!" Carly exclaimed, reaching for the designer luggage the young man was holding. He and a woman, his wife Carly presumed, entered the home with a big smile on their faces.

"Hello!" the young woman exclaimed. "We are so happy to be here!" She extended her hand and gave Carly a firm handshake. The young man followed with a sheepish grin across his face. Carly quickly checked their reservation and showed them to their room. This couple, Jason and Rachael Jones, were staying for the weekend. They were from Long Island, New York, and traveled a far distance by car and ferry. It was only 10 am, but they were probably ready to take a nap from waking up in the early hours of the morning. They were celebrating their third anniversary and wanted to spend a romantic weekend away.

Carly loved hearing about the lives of her visitors. Every story seemed so magical and more exciting than her own.

Carly had a total of four guests she needed to check-in today. Waiting for everyone to check in was the most challenging part of her day because of the uncertainty of when they would arrive. Carly preferred to go for a run, or grocery shopping, or work in her garden, but she had to make sure she was presentable and mentally prepared to greet and welcome all her guests.

Repeat customers and word of mouth made her business successful, and she needed to make sure that every experience was positive. That meant that no one had to wait when they arrived. Carly busied herself in the kitchen, making fresh blueberry muffins and coffee while she waited for the others.

Carly sat at the table, waiting for the timer on the microwave to ding. The sweet, warm smell was taunting her as she opened the oven. Carly thought of all the things she needed to do that week: pay the bills, shop, laundry, yardwork, visit her mother, and read reviews online. Her list didn't seem long, but it still caused her anxiety. Her anxiety always grew when she wasn't able to accomplish anything due to waiting around for guests. Carly took a deep breath and listened to the sound of the waves and the birds chirping, creating a melody of their own.

When Carly was a little girl, she dreamed of living away from the island. The constant lap of water against the shore soothed Carly, so she knew she needed to be near the ocean no matter where she lived. It helped clear the cobwebs of her mind when life seemed overwhelming.

Carly moved to Maine because she needed a change. She knew that Portland was small enough of a city that she wouldn't feel lost but big enough to make herself lost if needed. Every morning, Carly walked along the shoreline and watched the sunrise. She thought about her parents, and struggled with the guilt of leaving.

Carly met John, a lobster fisherman when she was twenty-eight. She waitressed at a quaint seafood restaurant in the middle of the city, and he delivered fresh lobsters throughout the week. Carly worked almost every day during the summer season and signed off on John's deliveries.

John was attractive, Carly decided, in a ruggedly rough way. He had long dark hair, a goatee and often wore cargo shorts and a t-shirt that was tight enough to accentuate the shape of his naturally toned arms and shoulders. John appeared to be a simple man.

Carly wasn't interested at first, but her attraction grew as she got to know him. She slipped him her phone number on a sticky note in the middle of July, and from that point forward, they were an item.

It happened fast, but they moved in together by December and stayed together until Carly's dad died. She knew she would have to make a difficult decision because Portland and Block Island were not a commutable distance. It would be a whole day of traveling between the ferry, the drive, and getting through Boston traffic, so they decided to take a break. Being a lobsterman was all John knew, and yes, Block Island was an island, but the lobster wasn't nearly as prevalent as it was in Maine.

That was nine years ago. They kept in touch for a while, but life moved fast, and eventually, they both moved on.

Carly thought about Maine often and wondered if John was still in the same apartment doing the same job with the same people. Probably not, she thought. Carly hoped that he found a woman and settled down. She hoped he was happy.

Carly's ringing phone snapped her out of her daydream down memory lane. "Willowside Inn," Carly spoke into the phone.

"Hi, can I please speak to the owners?" a deep voice on the other end of the line asked.

"This is Carly. How can I help you today?" Carly replied.

"Carly! Hey! It's Chris Swanson, your old neighbor." Carly immediately recognized his voice and imagined the eight-year-old boy riding his bike up and down the hills into town to get ice cream with her. They spent many days riding their bikes all over the island, solving mysteries that they created in their imagination.

Carly remembered the one time they were peeking into old Mrs. Crandell's living room window to find her staring back at them with her thin frame, dark beady eyes, and wild white hair. The two of them screamed in shock, jumped on their bikes, and rode home so fast that they collapsed in the driveway. Carly's parents made them write an apology note to Mrs. Crandell and promised they would never look in her windows again. Carly chuckled to herself at the memory. Chris moved off the island after high school to go to college and never returned. His parents sold their home for millions once all the kids moved out and they retired down south. Carly never saw him again.

"Wow! Chris! It's been years! How have you been?" she quickly responded.

Carly and Chris spoke for a while, catching up on island life. Who was still living? Who passed away? Why was she back? Carly didn't want to go into the entire story, so she told him that it was best for her family and the business. After a few minutes of chatting, Chris revealed the purpose of his phone call.

"Carly, I have a favor to ask you. A favor from one friend to another." Carly waited on the other end, not quite sure where this conversation was going. It had been almost twenty years since they last spoke or saw each other. What type of favor could she possibly do for him? "I know a girl," Chris continued, "who needs a place to stay for a while, and she can't afford summer rates. It's my girlfriend's sister."

"Why does she need a place to stay?" Carly interrupted him. "Is she in trouble with money or the law?" She laughed at the joke, but her thoughts immediately went to all the crime and law television shows she watched over the years. She imagined drugs, prostitution, teen pregnancy, or an abusive husband. There were so many potential reasons why someone needed a place to stay on a remote island.

"Oh, it's nothing like that!" Chris laughed. "She works for a paper, and they gave her a summer assignment to investigate island life around New England. She knew I was from Rhode Island, so she thought I might know someone who could help her out. She needs a place to stay."

A summer assignment, Carly thought. What exactly does that mean? She talked to Chris about the details. Her rooms were going for three hundred dollars a night on the weekends and two hundred seventy-five dollars a night during the workweek. That was a lot of money to throw away during the busiest time of the year. Chris convinced Carly that she wasn't going on vacation. She was going to immerse herself in island life. Chris pointed out that it could be a fantastic opportunity for her business to spread and grow. This reporter would be reporting on her experiences, and eventually, somewhere in her writing, she would name the place where she was staying and most likely review it.

Carly had to think about it. If she let a stranger stay in one of her rooms for the entire summer, she would lose too much money. She didn't even know if there would be room since reservations filled so far in advance. Carly couldn't have her staying in the main house. It was too risky, and if Carly was ever going to get off this island, she needed all the money she could get.

There was a carriage house set behind the main house that had been empty for years. Carly knew that if she ever got around to fixing it up, it would be a positive private addition to her business, but life seemed to get in the way, and the carriage house continued to sit. The house wasn't in great shape, but it did have walls, wooden floors, and an old bathroom straight out of the 1970s. Not up to tourism standards, but it could be livable with a bit of love. It could be perfect for our reporter, Carly thought, if she turned out to have a second identity or be a serial killer.

Carly told Chris that yes, Joanie could stay, but the accommodations weren't great and that she would need to help out around the bed and breakfast if she wanted to stay for free. Carly thought about the hours it took to wash all the linens when she could be doing something else. Grocery shopping in the small market with hundreds of tourists paralyzed by sticker shock was overwhelming. She spent too much time waiting for guests to arrive or check out when her to-do list grew by the second. Yes, Carly told Chris, this could be good. Carly had one week to clear all the debris and junk from the carriage house when her new roommate would arrive.

* * *

"You what?" Joanie looked at Chris's big smile and hugged him. She looked at her sister, Jackie, and said, "I cannot believe he did that." Chris contacted a girl whom he hadn't spoken to in twenty years for her. Joanie knew firsthand how difficult that must have been because how do you naturally start a conversation? Hello. I know it's been half our life, but can you spare a room for free for the summer? She could only imagine how awkward their conversation must have been.

Chris told her she had a week to pack a bag and get down there. He told her she was in the carriage house, which sounded very Victorian and romantic. Joanie could only imagine the big windows, stained glass, and birds chirping. Chris told her his friend was always busy. In high school, she was on the Yearbook committee, played sports, played an instrument, and was the first class president the school ever had for their measly graduating class of nine. To Joanie, Carly sounded like a nightmare. Well, at least she will have a whole building to herself, she thought, and contact should be minimal.

Joanie asked Chris if she would have to pay for the room, and he told her it was free for the summer. He mentioned that she would have to help out here and there, but Joanie thought that would be great material for her articles. Joanie planned on staying four consecutive days a week so she could check in on her plants, pop into the office, drop off her pieces, and make sure her team was working. Even if this were the worst experience of her life, Joanie thought, she would be home in eight weeks. All she had to do was get through July and August.

She met with Mark that afternoon and told him the assignment was a go. She told him she knew a guy who knew a girl so the newspaper wouldn't have to pay any money for her housing. She researched The Willowside Inn and felt comfortable with what she saw. A grand colonial home with white siding, black shutters, and a red door stood behind flowering trees and newly cut grass. Trees in the front yard provided ample shade for a swinging bench next to the house. A big black and white sign with the name in delicate letters sat in front of the house. The breakfast room had two tables set up with plain decor, and the rooms had a queen or king-size bed with fluffy pillows and bedsheets. It looked fancier than Joanie felt comfortable with, but she reminded herself that she wasn't staying in this house.

She searched for the owner and found a quick biography on Carly Davis. In her mid-thirties, Carly Davis wore her blonde hair, straight and long. Her white teeth and bright blue eyes welcomed Joanie instantly. Joanie clicked on the email link to introduce herself.

Hi Carly, Joanie typed. My name is Joanie Wilson, and Chris is my sister's boyfriend. I wanted to thank you for letting me stay with you this summer. I was wondering, is there anything I need to bring? Sheets, towels, or blankets? I know you are doing me a favor, so I am willing to do whatever you need to help. Thank you so much for everything. I can't wait to meet you! —Joanie. Joanie hit send and immediately questioned the use of the exclamation point. She wondered if it screamed desperation or enthusiasm.

She watered her plants and plucked off the dead leaves. Studies showed that speaking to your plants would help them live, and Joanie thought for sure that if her plants were ever going to be mad at her, it would be now. She thought of all the things she had to do before Friday. Joanie needed to go to the post office, put in a vacation hold, empty her trash, and leave on a light so no one would know she wasn't home. This is ridiculous, she thought. I am going away for four-day stretches, not four months. Joanie scratched the post office idea. Joanie took a deep breath, told herself it would be fine, and went into the office to tell Mark that she needed to meet with her team to discuss the summer.

Mark stood in his office with his hands against his waist, smiling down at her, sitting in the overstuffed black armchair. He couldn't believe that she found a place to live for free. This was better than he ever could have expected. When he initially assigned this assignment to Joanie, he thought it would be good to keep her engaged in the paper and possibly attract new readers. After she agreed, he thought about how different summer and winter life can be for the islands. He decided that if the paper was still around and this summer series was a success in terms of readership and followers, he would send her back in the winter to give his readers another perspective.

"Wonderful!" Mark clapped his hands. "Be sure to save all your receipts, including the ferry rides, food shopping, drinks when you go out to chat with the locals, and any island activities you do. Save everything. The paper will reimburse you on the 1st and the 15th of the month once you go over the cash advance." Joanie looked at him blankly. She didn't think about how she would survive out there in the middle of summer during the busiest, most expensive time. Joanie didn't have any money. She looked at the calendar and realized that July 1st was ten days away. She could probably survive the next ten days without using any of her own money. "Okay, thanks," she distractedly replied. She walked out of his office holding reimbursement forms and headed toward her cubicle.

On her desk was a small bouquet with a card signed by her team that said, "It's 5:00 somewhere." Joanie smiled to herself. She wished she was going to a tropical island somewhere where the water was clear, snorkeling was a thing to do, and the weather never dropped below 80. That type of place was not where she was going, but at least it was better than the summer in Boston.

Joanie rounded up the team members who were there and made her announcement. "You already know I took on a summer assignment on Block Island, but that does not mean I will not be around. I am always available via telephone or email. I will be checking into the office once a week to meet with you and make sure you have what you need. While I am gone, please go to Mikayla or Mark with any questions. They will be overseeing the print organization and will be assigning you your topics. You will send me your finished articles, and I will send everything to Mikayla to prepare the articles for printing. I might be in the office less, but I am still here, part of the team, and available if you need anything. Remember, I am just a ferry ride away." A ferry ride and a two-hour car ride, Joanie thought to herself, but who's counting? She thanked them for the flowers, packed up her contact list for the team and managers, her notebook, her lucky pen, and went home to pack. Ready or not, here I come, she thought.

Chapter 4

What was I thinking? Carly thought to herself. Why would I allow a stranger to stay at my house for free in the middle of the summer? If my parents were still around, they would kill me. Carly looked at the carriage house and sighed. She was overwhelmed by the mess and didn't even know where to begin. There was a bed, a dresser, a small kitchenette area, a couch, and a bathroom. It wasn't Buckingham Palace, but with a bit of love, it could be beautiful. Carly didn't have time or attention to focus on the carriage house, so the level of love she could give this place was minimal. This reporter, whom Carly couldn't remember her name, was arriving Monday. Thankfully Carly didn't have anyone else checking in until Friday.

The last time anyone stayed at this guest house was twenty years ago. Carly came home from Maine with her boyfriend, John. Her parents refused to allow them to stay in the same bedroom, so one of them had to stay in the carriage house. Sure, they weren't married, but they were living together, so what was the difference? Carly and John were broke. They could barely afford the ferry ride over or the gas to get home. Affording a room at another establishment was out of the question. John slept in the carriage house, and Carly slept on the couch in her parent's apartment.

It wasn't the visit she was expecting. Her father showed interest in John's work but told Carly he seemed a little rough around the edges. Peter questioned the dirty jeans, long beard, and scruffy hair. John sat on a fishing boat for months in the cold, windy water. He smelled like fish, which eventually became his regular scent.

Her mother didn't trust him. Carly's grandfather had been a fisherman off the coast of Block Island. Because of the lifestyle, the constant lack of sleep, and the stress of not knowing if there would be enough money to pay the rent or buy food, Carly's grandfather resorted to drinking his worries away. Drinking away his wages led to traditional Irish boiled dinners because it was all they could afford. In private, Ruth often asked Carly about John's drinking habits. Carly knew where the questions stemmed from, but it still bothered her that Ruth didn't trust her decision-making skills, especially when it came to a partner.

John stayed in the carriage house during their last trip home. It was a weekend full of tension, side-eye glances, and double intention sighs. Carly got tired of defending her boyfriend, so they left a day early.

This carriage house brought back many memories and emotions of that trip, and Carly needed to let it go. She was going to do her best to clean it up, make it acceptable, and welcome her guest with a clean, clutter-free space that didn't hold any memories.

Carly grabbed the linens on the bed and threw them into the donate pile. She grabbed the towels in the kitchenette and linen closet and smelled them. Mildew and dust seeped into her nostrils. She tossed them into the wash pile. The curtains faded to a lighter hue from the sun, and dust blanketed one side. The shower curtain was pea green with mildew climbing up the bottom. Carly shuddered as she ripped it down from the shower bar. She eliminated most of the décor and memories of her childhood.

Carly rewashed all the dishes and made a list of what she needed to buy at the store. She pulled everything off the walls, put them in the basement, vacuumed the rugs, dusted the surfaces, and sprayed every place you could sit or sleep.

After a long day, Carly sat down and looked around. The place could use a little paint, but there was no time for that. She looked at the pile of items to be donated and carried them down into the basement. There was no place to donate on the island, and there was no way she would transfer all the stuff to the mainland today. She brought all the trash to the dumpster and decided she did enough work for one day. Tomorrow she would spend time on the mainland, buying new décor and decorating the carriage house for her new roommate.

* * *

Joanie didn't know what to do. Do islanders own a car? Having a car transported to and from Block Island was rather expensive. If she didn't bring her car over, how in the world would she get home? Joanie did some research and found that bringing an automobile back and forth for the summer would cost her a few hundred dollars. She could also park her car at the port on the mainland, which would cost a little less, but she would be stuck on the island without a car. Of course, the paper was paying, but initially, Joanie was covering the cost. She would have to drop off her receipts for reimbursement immediately because she didn't have any extra money in her bank account.

Joanie's heart rate increased, and her palms sweated as she thought about driving a big car on a boat. It was too much for her brain to process. When she first learned to drive, she popped a tire, backed into a car while trying to park, and sideswiped a mirror while taking a turn too closely. She knew that if she sideswiped a car on the ferry, there would be no way to hide the fact that it was her who did it.

She thought about walking to the bed and breakfast and being trapped on an island for four days without a car and wondered which scenario was worse. Even if she had a car, what was she going to do? Drive along the bottom of the ocean until she came out on the other side? No, a car would not make sense. Parking in a parking lot for four days made her nervous as well, but she looked at her Teal Blue 2003 Saturn Ion and realized that if someone was going to steal a car, her car was not the one to take.

Joanie wondered what she should pack. She wanted to fit in and not look like a tourist because that was the whole point of her assignment. Joanie had been studying Block Island maps in her travel guide for days because the last thing she wanted to do was pull out her book while figuring out how to get from the dock to the bed and breakfast. She packed her bathing suit and towel because people go to the beach. Joanie threw in a pair of sneakers since bicycling would be her primary mode of transportation. Joanie hadn't ridden a bicycle since she was fourteen, so she packed a helmet just in case.

There were so many items she didn't already have that she needed for this trip. She bought new sneakers, sheets and a pillow for her bed, a bathing suit, and a new backpack for whatever day trips she found herself on. Joanie didn't trust other people's sheets and pillows. She used to stay up late at night watching videos on science topics, and one that especially freaked her out was about the dust mites and bugs that lived in your bedding.

She also upgraded her cell phone service because she had no idea how good the wi-fi or cell service was and didn't want to go over her data usage. After that costly trip to the store, Joanie decided to open up a separate bank account to track all her expenses.

She couldn't believe she was leaving in forty-eight hours! Jackie and Chris planned a celebratory dinner for later that night. Joanie's parents retired to Florida, so she texted them to let them know she was leaving on Tuesday. She occasionally texted them to let them know what was going on in her life, but they were often too busy to respond. They rarely texted back beyond the obligatory "Great," so Joanie didn't expect anything in return.

Excitement and exuberance spilled out of her. She couldn't believe how easily everything fell into place. Joanie threw on a red sundress that contrasted with her pale skin, pulled her red hair into a messy bun, and ran eyeshadow across her eyelids. In comparison to Jackie, she was Plain Jane, but this was her night, and she wasn't going to let her confidence fall because of her sister.

Joanie walked into the restaurant and found Chris and Jackie sitting at a small bistro table with three drinks in front of them. Jackie's red, curly hair was cascading down her back. Joanie could see all the hues and highlights reflecting off the overhead lights. She looked stunning in her white, fitted button-down shirt and black slacks. Her red lips matched her hair and contrasted with her bright blue eyes.

Joanie quickly scanned herself, questioning her outfit selection. She knew it was too late to run out the door and change, so she threw them her best smile and confidently walked toward the table.

"Joanie!" Jackie jumped up from the table and threw her arms around her older sister. "You look amazing!" she cried. It had been over half a year since they had last seen each other.

Joanie turned toward Chris and gave him an awkward hug. She didn't know him but knew that she was grateful for his generosity.

"Chris, tell me about Carly." Joanie sipped her margarita.

"She's cool," he responded. Joanie waited.

"And?" she probed.

"I don't know. She was cool when we were kids. Last I knew she was living in Maine. I didn't know that she came back. I don't know where her parents are. Maybe they died? She was desperate to get off that island and get away from her parents' control. When I called, I thought I would talk to her mom, but now that I think about it, her mom must be in her 80's."

Joanie listened to Chris tell stories about life on Block Island. How isolated he felt growing up, how everyone knew everyone, and how he felt like his childhood was under a microscope.

Joanie continued to sip her drink and tried to put herself in his shoes. She wondered if this vacation spot was as impressive as her mind made her believe or if she was desperate to escape her predictable, mundane life.

That night, she slept at Chris and Jackie's apartment, which was in a quaint neighborhood within walking distance of the water. Joanie had never been to her sister's apartment before, and the overall design of her decorating intrigued her. Joanie saw the clean, white walls in every room with perfectly centered, framed artwork hanging like an anchor that tied together all the furniture in the room. The furniture was simplistic and minimal, and there was no clutter to be seen. Joanie wondered where Jackie placed the piles of mail and magazines that came every day.

It lacked personality but seemed appropriate for Jackie.

"This place is cute!" Joanie lied. "I love this painting!" Joanie pointed toward the abstract art piece with swirls of color. It looked like something she made in grade school.

"Thanks!" Jackie replied. There is an art studio in Newport that I walk by every day to work, and I couldn't resist picking it up."

Joanie nodded, unsure of how to respond. "Thanks for letting me stay here," Joanie changed the subject.

Jackie walked her down a long, sterile hallway to a bedroom with a bed, a nightstand, a dresser, artwork above the bed, and three framed photos on the dresser top. It looked like something straight out of a hotel.

Jackie grabbed Joanie by the shoulders and said, "It's so nice to have you here." Joanie smiled, and Jackie pulled her into an awkward hug and then left the room.

They gravitated to the couch, drinking red wine and talking about the move.

"Are you excited?" Jackie asked. "I would love to come to visit sometime!"

"I am, yes! I'll text you once I get settled and scope the place out. Maybe you could come for a day trip or something," Joanie appeased.

"Chris and I are driving out to see Mom and Dad in August, but maybe we can come out before then."

Joanie took a rather large gulp of wine. "Do you talk to Mom and Dad often?"

"Maybe once or twice a week. Enough to stay in touch. It helps me, knowing that they are still alive. If I didn't call them, I don't think they would ever call me. I usually call to check-in."

Of course. Jackie was always the better daughter, Joanie thought. She was the one who got good grades, did all her chores, and made thoughtful gifts for the family, just for fun. Of course, she made an effort to keep in touch. Joanie took another gulp of wine and remembered why she and her sister weren't close.

"How are they?" Joanie asked. "I haven't spoken to them since Christmas." She quickly added, "I did send them cards for Mother's Day and Father's Day." If Jackie picked up on the competitive statement, she didn't let it affect her.

"Oh, you know. They love being retired. Dad golfs, mom paints. I think the south fits them."

"Do you remember that time when Mom and Dad caught us with all that beer in our car? For the summer music festival?" It was one of the fonder memories Joanie had with her sister. "You bailed me out."

"Yes!" Jackie turned toward Chris. "I was seventeen, and Joanie was almost twenty. I convinced Joanie to come with my friends and me to this all-day music festival. The plan was to tailgate in the parking lot and then let the alcohol burn off throughout the day. Some of Joanie's friends were twenty-one, so she got ahold of a couple of thirty-packs. Mom and dad somehow figured out that something was up."

Joanie interrupted, "I think it was because we never really hung out before, so it was weird that we were going to this concert together. I wanted to go because I loved the bands, but all my friends were busy. Jackie wanted to go because she wanted to get wasted with all her friends. I was the designated driver."

"When we were leaving, Mom and Dad asked Joanie to open the trunk."

"Yes! I wanted to drive away as quickly as possible, but I had to open it." Joanie added.

"They found the beer and gave Joanie a look. We watched them put the beer in the garage and then told us we could leave. They probably thought not having the beer and being at this music festival sober was punishment enough." Jackie continued, "We drove around town, trying to figure out how to get more beer before leaving for the show."

"We ended up driving back home," Joanie interrupted again. "Dad was mowing the lawn, and mom was nowhere in sight. We parked on the side of the house, which had huge, overgrown shrubs blocking the view from the window. Jackie sneaked past dad and tiptoed into the garage, which was still open. She grabbed the cases of beer, ran back to the car, and we took off like a speeding bullet."

"Mom and Dad eventually noticed the beer was gone but never really asked us what happened. They never saw a thing." Jackie and Joanie laughed at the memory.

"They never found out, but they secretly held me responsible," Joanie said. "I think that was the start of our relationship falling away."

Chris laughed at the story. "I had no idea you guys were close as kids!" he said.

"We weren't. That was probably the first time we had hung out since Joanie left for college. We hung out that summer, and then I went to college. We lost touch. Life got complicated and busy," Jackie said.

Sadness hung over Joanie because Jackie's words were valid. Life got complicated. Joanie never took the time to show any interest in Jackie's life. Now, almost twenty years later, she was sitting in her sister's home for the first time.

Joanie took another gulp of wine, hoping that her excitement for Block Island would crush the sadness of another lost opportunity that she created.

* * *

On Monday, Mark organized a farewell luncheon. Joanie drove to the office with an extra pep in her step and a big smile across her face. Excitement for change motivated Joanie to keep a positive attitude.

The office was dark and eerily quiet. People were there, but they weren't exactly working. They were mingling around the water cooler, standing in the cubicles, or quietly talking amongst themselves. Joanie smiled brightly and waved. Her colleague, Rebecca, waved back but didn't return the smile. Joanie looked around and found a table spread of sandwiches, donuts, juice, coffee, tea, and picnic salads. All the boxes and platters were full. Balloons floated against the ceiling, and streamers draped down the door frames.

"Where is Mark?" Joanie asked Rebecca. Rebecca discreetly motioned in the direction of his office, trying to communicate the moment's mood with her eyes.

"Joanie! Hello!" Mark greeted her as she approached his office.

"Hi, Mark. What's going on? Everyone's acting as if someone died out there."

"Oh, that. Yes. Well," Mark started but couldn't quite finish a sentence. He shoved an envelope containing a transfer slip toward her and said, "Here you go. This is for you. I just transferred some money into your account. Keep your receipts, and please try not to spend the money all at once. It is a 500-dollar cash advance. That should be enough to get you started. Everything is reimbursable." Joanie took the thick envelope and placed it in her handbag. "Okay," he continued, "Let's go eat!"

Joanie and Mark approached the table as he tried to get everyone's attention. "Ahh-hem!" He clapped his hands loudly over his head. Everyone turned and waited for his announcement. "I would like to thank Joanie for taking on this assignment to write about life on Block Island. We will miss having her here at the office daily but know that she will still be here, ready and willing to keep the Lifestyle section afloat. If you have any questions throughout the week, please do not hesitate to contact Mikayla or me. Joanie may or may not have cell phone service. Please enjoy this luncheon on behalf of the office to wish Joanie the best of luck. Cheers." Mark raised his cup as if he was giving her a toast at her wedding. Everyone continued to mumble under their breaths before placing the dirty dishes back on the table. Mark was back in his office.

"What's going on?" Joanie asked Mikayla. "Everyone seems …worried." Mikayla shrugged her shoulders. "The threat of everyone losing their job in a few months is bringing us all down. I think people are ready to jump ship. I've gotten so many emails from other magazines and newspapers asking if people work here. I think they're just worried that in a few months, they are going to be jobless."

Joanie listened to Mikayla's words and let the gravity of the situation weigh on her shoulders. Here she was, going to a vacation destination when really, she should be looking for a job. Joanie assumed that Mark would save her career. Whether the company survived or died, Joanie thought that she would still be here. Maybe she should have been a little more aware of the what-ifs.

Chapter 5

Carly was scrambling around the foyer, making sure everything was ready for the guests coming in for the weekend. She found it hard to keep the bed and breakfast decor completely neutral and lacking any personality. Looking around, it would be impossible to determine if a woman or a man resided in the home. When her parents actively ran The Willowside, the decor was straight out of the Victorian era. Now that Carly was in charge, the furniture was straight out of IKEA. Clean lines, a modern feel, and a pop of color here and there brought the house to life. She was hoping that the contemporary decor would attract a younger crowd.

Carly scanned the parlor, carried the old, expired magazines into the kitchen, and dropped them into the trash bin. She sat at the kitchen table with a hot cup of tea and waited for the doorbell to ring. Today she was expecting three new couples. Two reserved until Sunday, and one reserved until Monday. A family of three booked the inn for a wedding and decided to turn it into a vacation. They were leaving Wednesday.

Joanie was scheduled to arrive later that day. Carly thought the carriage house looked reasonably clean and welcoming. She communicated with Chris throughout the week, hoping that the changes she made to the carriage house were adequate for Joanie. Carly even placed a bicycle she found in the garage outside the door so that Joanie could get around the island quickly. She still wondered if she was crazy allowing someone to stay for free during the busiest time of the year.

After lunch, Carly watered the flower beds. Jonah, a boy that Carly went to high school with, drove up in his cab and out stepped a plain, frumpy woman in baggy jeans, a button-down blouse, and sensible loafers. Her short straight hair had a bandana wrapped around the perimeter of her head. She walked toward Carly carrying a backpack and a weekender bag, stuck out her hand, and said, "Hi, I'm Joanie." Carly returned the handshake and noticed the clamminess to her palm. Carly wiped her palm on her jeans and introduced herself. They walked to the carriage house so Joanie could drop off her stuff.

Joanie didn't make eye contact or share any information about herself. Carly led her into the guest house and told her she would check in with her in a few hours to see if she needed anything. Carly thought about Chris and how he made it seem like this would be a great idea. Now, here she was with a person who couldn't even look at her, let alone hold a conversation.

Carly tried to let the awkward exchange roll off her shoulders, but this was not what she had anticipated. She was hoping for someone like her: friendly, talkative, enthusiastic, and personable. Instead, Joanie was introverted, quiet, and maybe rude if Carly really thought about it. Joanie did say thank you, but it didn't seem genuine to Carly.

Carly emailed Chris to let him know that Joanie arrived. She needed to be careful with what she said and how she said it because Chris was dating her sister. Any negativity could easily get back to Joanie. Carly knew that Joanie's purpose was to immerse herself in island life, but Carly had a feeling it would not be easy with her social skills. Carly decided to give her the benefit of the doubt and help her however she could. Maybe she would be Joanie's tour guide for the next few days by showing her where things were and introducing her to people within the community.

Carly walked back over to the carriage house and told Joanie that she wanted to take her around once settled and unpacked. Joanie came over to the bed and breakfast an hour later. They walked into town instead of riding bikes because Carly thought it would be easier to chat.

"So, how was your trip?" Carly asked. They could see the ocean in the far distance and the businesses of the main drag down below.

"It was good. I didn't realize how long it would take to get here from Boston. I was up at four and got off the ferry at twelve. I can't imagine doing that every few days."

Carly smiled and replied, "Well, you made it safe and sound, and hopefully, the next trip will be easier." After a few seconds of silence, Carly continued, "Chris told me a little bit about your work. Are you a reporter? What exactly are you writing about while staying here?" Carly thought if she knew what type of articles Joanie was writing, she could set her up with the right people. There were less than 1,000 year-round islanders and thousands and thousands of tourists every summer. If Joanie didn't know who to look for, she could be chatting up with tourists all summer long.

Joanie thought for a moment before responding. "I'm writing one article a week about life on the island. I need to focus on one area of island life per week. Maybe interview a few people, get to know the ins and outs of the industry, and throw in my impression of life on Block Island." There was an awkward pause, and Joanie quickly added, "Thank you for the room. That saved me!"

"No problem." Carly thought about the different "industries" Joanie mentioned. "You could interview me. I work year-round, and winter is completely different than summer. I could represent a hospitality job. I can introduce you to everyone on the main drag, and maybe you could interview a small business owner. My second cousin is on the police force. Maybe I can see if he is available. And my dad's best friends' kids are still local fishermen. How many articles do you have to write?"

"Six," Joanie said. "The first week will be about my transition here, and the last will be a wrap-up. Is there a teacher I can interview? Also, I wanted to speak to a local farmer, if there is one," she said, looking off into the distance, embarrassed by her lack of research prior to arriving.

As they entered the fish and chips shop, they created a plan. Carly had some work to do to set up all these interviews. To buy some time, they decided Joanie would attack the hospitality section first. She wanted Joanie to feel successful and believed that having a willing, open interviewee, such as herself, would start her on the right foot.

When they got home from their walk, Carly made some phone calls. She decided the best way for Joanie to meet everyone was to have a casual party. It would be difficult to host people when guests were staying at the house, but Carly was a master planner. The Willowside sat on two acres of land, and the carriage house remained behind the main house, so entertaining people behind the carriage house would probably be fine. They would be so far away from the main inn, the guests wouldn't even know people were over.

Carly knew that Joanie was heading back next Tuesday, and she needed her first article done for Friday. Carly contacted everyone on Joanie's wish list and invited them over Sunday evening for a bonfire, hamburgers, and dogs. Once they were all invited, Carly focused her attention on the party details.

* * *

Joanie sat on the oversized floral couch and stretched out her legs. She hadn't walked that far since college, and her body was silently screaming at her. The carriage house definitely needed some love, but she wasn't picky. Joanie sipped a chilled glass of lemonade and looked around the room. The kitchen was olive green with Formica countertops and a brown cracked vinyl floor. The stained rug from too many years of neglect peeled up on the corners, and Joanie moved the end table so she wouldn't trip on it.

Despite the old fixtures, the decorations themselves were new. Joanie assumed that Carly spent some time updating the place for her visit. The blanket on the bed had a chevron design, and the sheets, blankets, and curtains all matched. The bathroom had new rugs and matched the shower curtain and sink accessories.

Joanie texted Mark and informed him that she arrived safely. She summarized her plan for the next few weeks. She requested a meeting on Wednesday to discuss her plans further. She then set up an appointment with her team to review the weekend Lifestyle section. Everything had to be ready by Friday for printing.

Joanie looked at her phone, waiting. Mark sent her back one word: Okay. Usually, when he responded with one word, he was busy or distracted, but he always told her what was interfering with their conversation. He might have said, "Hey, so and so is on the phone. Text you later." This time all she got was "Okay."

She blamed it on the cell service at Block Island. Thankfully the island was close enough to the coast of Rhode Island so the cell waves could travel, but the quality of the cell waves might deteriorate with the weather. She looked outside and saw sunny skies.

Joanie sat outside the carriage house and paid attention to her senses. The sky was blue with few clouds, the grass was green, the beach was rocky and had lots of cliffs, and the only sounds filling the space were birds chirping. A handful of cars roamed around the island, and the hum of the engines barely audible.

Joanie pulled out her notebook and wrote down the occupations of the people she was hoping to interview. She knew minimal information about each of them. Attached to her notebook was a calendar that Joanie needed to set up the interviews. She had already blocked out the boxes when she would be returning home to Boston. Her calendar was half empty, and half blocked. Not a bad summer, Joanie thought to herself.

When Joanie was a kid, her parents took her and her sister to Cape Cod on vacation. Joanie and Jackie built elaborate sand villages on the sandy beaches. Included in their beach toys were dolls and animals that made their world come to life. Jackie was eighteen months younger than Joanie, but most strangers assumed they were twins. They both had red, curly hair as children, deep chestnut eyes, and fair, freckled skin.

Jackie didn't know it, but Joanie followed her lead when playing with other kids and talking to others. Joanie never knew what to say, and she always felt awkward and uncomfortable in her skin. Jackie was the outgoing, mischievous one, while Joanie was the quiet, introspective one. Joanie always wanted to be more like Jackie.

When high school hit, everyone knew Jackie. The smart kids, the jocks, the stoners, the musicians, and all the teachers knew her name. Joanie became known as "Jackie's sister." She often felt forgotten even though she was older and had been through school first. No matter how hard she tried, she was constantly within her sister's shadow. She borrowed Jackie's clothes without asking, had Jackie do her hair and makeup for dances, and tagged to the movies with Jackie and her friends on Friday nights.

As they got older, the gap between them widened, and now they barely talked. It was ironic how little the two women spoke, yet they logistically lived near each other.

Joanie hopped on her bike and started riding. She carried her notebook and pencil in the basket in front of the bike and decided to get lost. When she was a kid, she rode her bike through their old neighborhood, hoping to find new sights. Instead of getting scared, her imagination took over, and she transported herself into a world of curiosity and mystery. She always made her way back home, even without the aid of a cell phone, and her mother never knew that she created an alternate universe where she often lived.

Joanie knew she wouldn't get lost because of technology and cell phones today, but she thought that if she fell off the beaten path, her observations would create authenticity to her writing to help sell newspapers.

The scenery was beautiful. The green hills, isolated homes, and rocky cliffs transported Joanie to a majestic land. She rode into town, through the touristy crowds, and out the other side. She rode along the beach and watched the sun fall into the ocean. The oranges, reds, and pinks filled the sky and reflected off the calm blue of the waves. Joanie kept going. The island itself was only seven miles long. Although she would get tired, there was no way she would get lost.

Once she left the downtown strip, she quickly ended up in a remote part of the island. Fewer cars, fewer people, and the random stray dog shared the narrow, windy road toward the beach. Joanie pulled her bike to the side of the road and hiked down to the water. She sat on the beige sand and looked out at the ocean. She listened to the waves lap against the rocks, watched the birds circle the water searching for food, and smelled the salt traveling through the air. It was beautiful and peaceful and put Joanie at ease.

Joanie knew she had to be chatty, friendly, and social during the cook-out this weekend. Her hands sweated and a lump formed in the back of her throat, thinking about the awkward interactions. She told herself it was only a few hours of her life. Joanie closed her eyes and focused on her five senses. For now, she was just going to watch the sun slowly set and listen to the waves lap against the rocks. The beauty surrounded her, and her nerves calmed.

Chapter 6

Carly ran around the kitchen, collecting all the condiments. With overfilled arms, she nudged the screen door open with her hip. She reached out to everyone on her list and invited them over for an early cook-out. It was a bizarre group of people. Carly knew some of them well and some of them not so well. Thankfully, they all agreed to come, even the few who only knew her name and her business.

Her second cousin, Matt, wasn't surprised to hear from her. He usually stopped over at the inn to check her smoke alarms and carbon monoxide detectors. He was Carly's age and had left the island after high school. He moved to the mainland to attend the Rhode Island Police Academy. Carly remembered how heartbroken his parents were when he left because they didn't believe he would return.

Matt had a bit of culture shock when he left. He suddenly could drive wherever he wanted whenever he wanted. He didn't have to check the ferry schedule. He could stop at a coffee shop and not run into anyone familiar. It was a wonderful break from reality but always left him feeling uneasy.

Matt graduated with Honors from the police academy and got a job as a patrolman in Providence. After a few years, he returned home. He lived at his parents' house, helped tend to the property, and eventually got a job with the police department. Vacancies were few and far between because the population was small and crime was low. Officers never retired, but when they did, the department struggled to find a qualified applicant.

Matt fell into a position less than a year after returning home. His parents both passed away, and Matt inherited their property. This type of transaction was common on Block Island because families that settled there originally passed down their property from generation to generation.

Lucas and Logan Brown were coming to the cookout also. Their father, Michael, was the local fisherman who delivered to all the eating establishments on the island. He provided fresh fish to the inn every week.

During Lent, Carly's Catholic family didn't eat meat, and Michael would drop off whatever fish remained after he delivered the local orders. Michael was a little younger than Carly's father, Peter, and Peter always wanted a son. They became fast friends, and Michael taught Peter how to fish. Michael passed away, but he taught his two sons to catch fish and run a business. They still had relationships with all the companies on the island. When tourism was down or when it was offseason, they continued to deliver to locals.

Mrs. Stanley was Carly's teacher during high school. Each student got the same coursework, but maybe not during the same year of education. It was the most cost-effective way to run the school.

Carly graduated with a class of nine, and her entire high school had forty-five kids. Carly dreamed of living somewhere else, where childish behavior didn't hang over you like a scarlet letter.

Mrs. Stanley was one of two teachers in her high school. She was now in her seventies and still working. Carly wasn't sure how effective her teaching was because she had become hard of hearing as the years continued. Mrs. Stanley gladly agreed to come to the party. She lived on the island alone and loved to connect with old students.

The most uncomfortable exchange was with the beekeepers, Andrew and Sara Cohen. The Cohen's inherited some land from a great aunt and moved to Block Island about four years prior from upstate New York. In New York, they took care of beehives and processed and sold honey for farmer's markets. They were in their thirties and did not have any children, so they ventured to Block Island, where they lived mortgage-free. Thankfully, the property they inherited was on six acres, which was plenty of room to set up their beehives. The Cohen's had a store downtown selling honey, but they also traveled to the mainland to expand their name at various farmer's markets. Carly thought it would be good for Joanie to get some perspective from an outsider trying to live on Block Island.

When Carly called, the Cohen's had no idea who she was or why she was calling. Carly loved to talk to people in person but struggled with telephone exchanges because body language and facial expressions were absent. Those things helped Carly decipher the meaning behind their words. Carly stumbled over her words and her explanation but finally communicated her message. Sara agreed to come over and volunteered to bring some delicious honey. Carly graciously accepted and told Sara that she couldn't wait to incorporate their honey into her cooking.

Carly placed a vinyl pineapple tablecloth on the table while waiting for everyone to arrive. Joanie prepared all the food and drinks inside. They decided that having the food mostly inside would be best if the weather shifted, as it often did. Joanie thanked Carly for organizing the day, but Carly could tell that Joanie was uncomfortable. She seemed to be trying to keep busy and be helpful with the setup but was chattering, asking many questions, and forgetting actually to do what Carly asked of her. Joanie admitted that she struggled with meeting new people, and Carly wondered how she even got into journalism.

Carly extended the invitation to the guests at the inn that weekend. The three sets of guests were already outside, drinking and sitting around the empty fire pit. They chatted about where they wanted to go and what they wanted to see during their vacation. Although they were just visitors, she thought it would have been rude not to include them. Plus, if Joanie truly struggled with small talk, then maybe the guests would be a good buffer. They didn't know anyone either, and maybe through conversation, Joanie would pick up on some information to ask more questions to the locals.

Ding! Carly ran to the door to find the Cohen's, of all people, first to arrive. "Hello! Welcome!" she exclaimed.

"Hi, Carly! Thank you for inviting us! We brought you some honey. It tastes delicious with pita chips! We were wondering if you could put some out for everyone to try?" Sara pushed a jar of honey into Carly's chest.

Carly smiled and said, "Of course! Follow me into the kitchen." As she poured the honey into a small bowl, she introduced Sara and Andrew to Joanie. Joanie stuck out her hand and said, "Hello! My name is Joanie. It is so nice to meet you!" The Cohen's tried to engage in small talk, but Joanie responded with short answers that didn't help maintain or expand their topic of conversation. After an awkward pause, Carly jumped in and explained why Joanie was on the island. Joanie smiled and followed the Cohen's into the yard. Her shoulders tightened, and her gait stiffened. Carly knew she felt uncomfortable just being there.

All the other guests trickled in slowly. Some brought side dishes or desserts, and some came empty-handed. Once the food was out, Carly looked out the kitchen window at the random group of people she assembled. Some islanders, some visitors, and one reporter who had a notebook and pen ready to jot down any pertinent information that came up in conversation milled around the firepit. Carly thought she should go out there and help Joanie but decided to watch everything unfold. She did Joanie a favor by organizing this random group of people and picnic. If Joanie worked in journalism, she could figure out how to talk to people.

* * *

The number of unfamiliar faces overwhelmed Joanie, but she knew that time was not on her side, and she had a deadline. She took a deep breath and approached a man who looked to be in his mid-forties. He had short, dark, wavy hair and a speckled white beard. His face certainly wasn't wrinkled, but lines of worry gave it depth. "How is the dip?" Joanie asked, nodding her head toward the plate he was holding.

The man turned to face her and eyed her up and down. "Good," he replied.

Joanie waited for more, but nothing else came. "Today is a beautiful day," she said, raising her eyes toward the sky.

"Sure is," the man replied.

Joanie waited again. Nothing. This conversation was more challenging than she thought. "My name is Joanie. I am staying in Carly's guest house for a few weeks," she introduced herself and stuck out her hand. The man took it and introduced himself as Matt. He explained that he was related to Carly and worked for the police force.

Joanie gave him her biggest smile and told him she was writing weekly articles for the Boston Tribune about island life. "I would love to sit down with you over a cup of coffee and talk about your experiences!"

They awkwardly conversed about the job, the crime, the gratitude of the locals, and the challenges island life presented. Joanie couldn't help but notice his dark hair, healthy build, and blue eyes. One of his dimples winked every time he smiled. His brow furrowed when he was deeply engaged in conversation. Joanie didn't know much about being a police officer on an island, and she clumsily led the discussion. Matt's tall, lean frame and penetrating eyes caused her thoughts to jumble.

Joanie looked down at her notes and realized she only had enough information for half her required word count. She dug for more. She needed to know the ins and outs of the job but wanted more anecdotal stories Matt told. Those stories allowed her to look into his soul without being too forward.

"Excuse me," a man tapped her on the shoulder. He was one of the guests staying at the house. "Do you have any more honey? It tastes delicious with these chips," the man held out an empty bowl with a coating of stickiness at the bottom.

"Absolutely!" Joanie exclaimed with a grin on her face. She got so caught up in Matt's stories that she forgot she needed to network with all of these people. "Excuse me." Joanie turned to Matt and sauntered off into the kitchen, hoping that he watched her sashay away. Focus, she told herself. Focus. Joanie filled the bowl with honey, set it on the table, and decided to approach Mr. and Mrs. Cohen next.

Joanie internally practiced various ways to interrupt their conversation politely. Excuse me. Hi, I'm Joanie! That is some excellent honey! Joanie shook her head. Maybe she should just laugh when they laughed, she thought to herself. Joanie knew she should have gone into business and not marketing or journalism because talking to people was too complicated to manage.

"Your honey is delicious! All the guests agree," Joanie blurted to the couple. They turned toward her and smiled.

"Thank you. It's organic and homegrown." Sara responded.

"I would love to buy some off of you. It is delicious!" Joanie stumbled.

"Of course. I am Sara," Sara said, holding out her hand.

Joanie took her hand and shook it, realizing that the honey from the jar dripped down her fingers. She thought she wiped it off, but the sticky residue remained. Sara immediately pulled away and grabbed a towel. Joanie escaped to the bathroom to wash her hands and snuck back outside through the side door. Joanie put the Cohen's on the bottom of her list for who to contact next.

Next, Joanie approached Mrs. Stanley, a cute older woman who reminded Joanie of her grandmother. Mrs. Stanley's white curly hair blew in the gentle breeze. It appeared she had gotten her hair set that day. She sat near the fire alone and quietly observed the guests.

Joanie sat next to her and said hello. Mrs. Stanly didn't turn her head or acknowledge her. Joanie didn't know what to do, so she cleared her throat and said hello louder. Still no response. She knew she looked like a crazy person talking to herself. She heard a quiet voice behind her say, "She can't hear you." Joanie turned to find Matt grinning from ear to ear.

Joanie rose, so her back faced Mrs. Stanley, and she whispered, "Thank you! I was about to get up and tap her on the shoulder!"

"Hey, Matt!" a young man with blonde, wavy hair approached them. Mrs. Stanley turned and smiled, and the young man waved. He turned to Matt and said, "Do you need any bass? We have a catch that no one ordered if you need some."

"Logan, this is Joanie. Have you met?" When Logan shook his head, Matt said, "Joanie, this is Logan." They smiled and shook hands professionally. Logan seemed friendly with kind eyes and a gentle smile. Joanie decided she would interview him after Matt.

They chatted back and forth about the seas, the weather, and the type of fish common to Block Island. Joanie asked if they could meet up for coffee sometime so she could work on her articles. They exchanged numbers and made a tentative date for next week.

Joanie roamed around the group, listening in on conversations, helping Carly refill food and drinks, and then cleaning up once all the guests left. She couldn't thank Carly enough for throwing this gathering together. Although she didn't hit it off with everyone, she could connect faces with names, which made the next contact just a little bit easier.

Carly smiled and told Joanie that she would help her get ready for the interviews and coffee dates. Joanie thanked Carly because it provided her more background information to help the interviews run smoothly. As long as Joanie had some input, she could prepare her interview questions in advance.

The next day, Joanie met Matt at the only coffee shop in town to get more information about his work. She told him she needed to meet the next day because her article was due soon. It wasn't a complete lie. Joanie stayed up most of the night thinking about his muscular physique, mysterious eyes, and perfectly fitting jeans. She found herself wondering if he had a girlfriend and blushed at thinking about the possibilities if the answer was no.

They met for coffee, and conversation surprisingly happened naturally. Joanie listened intently to his answers, inferred that he was single, liked his job, and communicated with Carly frequently. Joanie knew that he came around the inn every few weeks. Joanie gulped her coffee down and asked the waitress for a refill. She didn't want the conversation to end.

Matt looked at his watch. "I have to get going soon. I have a shift this afternoon." Joanie sat at the table with her hot cup of coffee as Matt excused himself. They didn't discuss seeing each other again, which disappointed Joanie. She assumed that he only met with her to complete her article, and she accepted that she might not ever see him again. On an impulse, Joanie grabbed the pen the waitress had left on the table and touched Matt's arm to get his attention.

Her body stiffened up, and she felt his arms tense at her touch. They locked eyes, and Joanie started fumbling. "Um, I, uh, I was wondering if we could exchange numbers." She felt a warmth run up her neck to her forehead and smiled nervously. "Just in case there was any information I still needed to verify or add," she added. "Or if you wanted to share some other information with me, you can."

Her eyes fell to the table, not quite sure how he would interpret that last sentence. He hesitated and then quickly wrote down his number on a napkin, and she did the same.

"I look forward to hearing from you," he said. She smiled up at him, shoved his napkin into her bag, and watched him leave.

Joanie eventually made her way back to the carriage house. The next day she returned to Boston. Joanie had a meeting set up with Mark and her team to ensure that the Lifestyle section was ready to be printed. She hadn't even written her first article yet, and she began to panic.

Joanie pulled out her laptop, sat in the wicker chair on the front porch, and started writing about her experiences coming to a small island off the coast of Rhode Island. She decided to format her first article like a journal entry to connect to her readers on a personal level. Joanie planned to write about the community of people, the scenery, and how her first week unfolded. She hoped her personality shined through the words and encouraged her readers to follow her throughout the summer. Maybe she could save the paper. If not, maybe she could save her job.

Chapter 7

Joanie walked into the office, which was abuzz with chatter and people moving from cubicle to cubicle. Phones rang, papers rustled, and computers pinged with email notifications. The sun penetrated brightly through the open blinds, and the shadows of her colleagues danced along the floor.

"How is everything?" Joanie asked Marley, the woman next to her desk. "It seems like a big story just broke." Joanie looked around the room and tried to read facial expressions. Few smiles were present, and the giddiness of the office was muted.

"Geez, Joanie! Did you see the news?" Joanie shook her head, feeling like an imposter. She lived in a place with no cable and spotty internet. She was lucky if she got local weather, let alone actual news. She arrived late last night and fell asleep within moments. She woke with a start to her alarm buzzing beside her, so, no, she didn't see the news.

Joanie turned on her phone. She didn't have any text messages from anyone important. Nothing from Mark, and she was supposed to be meeting with him in ten minutes. "No, actually, I haven't. What's up?" Marley raised her eyebrows as if to say, What a great manager you are! She pulled up the local news station on her computer. On the homepage, it read, Boston Paper Bought out by Chicago Media Giant in big letters.

"Oh shit," Joanie mumbled under her breath. She quickly scanned the article, but Joanie didn't find pertinent information.

"Where's Mark?" Joanie frantically looked around the room. Her eyes narrowed as she recognized his dark, empty office.

"I don't know. We haven't seen or heard from him at all," Marley responded. She sat at her desk and sighed heavily. Marley picked up the picture of herself, her husband, and her two small children and turned it upside down. "What am I going to do if I lose my job?" Marley placed her head in her hands.

Joanie felt safe from the transition because she was a manager, but Marley was just a first-level associate. She took care of the classifieds, which most people didn't even use anymore. Joanie silently agreed that Marley's position would probably be eliminated and threw her a sympathetic glance.

"Don't worry, Marley. Until we talk to Mark, we don't know what is going to happen." Joanie pulled out her phone and texted Mark. Mark, call me. The office is a mess. I need to know what is going on. Where are you? She hit send and waited. A blank screen stared back at her. She put her phone face up on her desk and turned the silence function off.

She opened her email, searching for clues. Nothing stood out as unordinary. She searched for information about the sale. A list of articles opened, but none of them gave any specific information. One report stated that the paper could lose up to 70% of its workforce. The only good thing, thought Joanie, was that the new owner was out of Chicago, so it was unlikely that she would automatically lose her job.

Joanie laughed to herself. Her chuckles turned into giggles which turned into cackles which turned into sobs. She didn't care that people in the office stopped and looked to see what was wrong or funny. The irony that they, a media company, were not notified of the sale of their own company until other media companies reported the deal was hysterically sad. She felt like all their credibility was gone.

As Joanie sorted through her thoughts, people approached her with questions: August 1st is only three weeks away. When will they be notified if they still have a job? How will this impact retirement? Should they keep working on their assignments? Where was Mark?

Joanie had no idea how to answer their questions, so she just smiled and said, "Mark will be here soon."

She didn't know if or when he would show up. He should have been here, holding the office together when the news broke. He blew off her meeting, which was not like him at all. Joanie suggested they continue working as if it were just another day. She told them to email her their questions and promised the anxious staff that she would get their answers.

Joanie knew today would be unproductive. People wouldn't be able to work as if nothing happened. Most of the staff lived paycheck to paycheck. She knew most of them would search and apply for new jobs because the potential outcome was too much to consider.

Throughout the day, Joanie checked her phone, but no messages waited for her. She checked her watch, her phone, and her email repeatedly. She had eighty-eight new emails intended for Mark. She knew she should be reading and jotting down concerns for her friends and colleagues, but the responsibility was too much for her. She looked in her purse for change so she could grab a candy bar from the vending machine. No one was working. She looked at her watch again.

She had two more hours to go and knew if she left and showed defeat, the entire office would also leave and feel defeated. She knew if they left defeated, they might never return. They needed each other, and Joanie wouldn't allow herself to be the one who set the resignation ball rolling. Instead, she continued to google, research, and check emails. By the end of the day, there was still nothing from Mark.

* * *

Carly hopped on the ferry with an overnight bag filled with clean laundry to drop off at her mom's facility. Every Wednesday, Carly made the trek into the mainland to check in on her mom, where they usually visited for a few hours. Carly ate lunch with Ruth, put her clothes away, picked up her dirty clothes, and watched the news with her. Sometimes her mom knew who she was, and other times, it was like they had just met for the first time. When her mom was confused by Carly's presence, Carly often played along, praying that her mom wouldn't snap into a lucid moment. When that happened, Ruth got upset and confused and then agitated and combative. Carly felt guilty for making her mom feel inferior or stupid when she was only trying to protect her.

Carly looked out at the blue waves. She stood on the top deck of the ferry and breathed in the salty air. The wind pushed her hair back, which allowed the sun to beat down on her fair skin. The hour ride allowed Carly to reflect on the past week, month, year, and life. She knew she would have to care for her parents one day, but she never realized how much sacrifice was in lost time and money. Thankfully, the inn did not accept new patrons on Wednesdays, which allowed a day for the cleaning woman to come in and upkeep the bed and breakfast. Carly was grateful that she could see her mom and not feel guilty about neglecting her business.

The ferry traveled to New London, Connecticut, which was a much bigger city than the small towns that dotted the Rhode Island coast. Carly did not take a car on the ferry because the expense was exorbitant. On a nice day, she walked to the nursing home, which overlooked the ocean. If her mother were in a facility inland, she would be miserable. The sea was what kept her grounded throughout her life. Carly coordinated a room with a view for a little extra money. When her mother was in a lucid state, they sat outside and watched the waves lap against the coast.

Carly exited the ferry and walked down the bustling streets that ran parallel to the Long Island Sound. Even though it was practically July, the humidity broke, and a nice breeze pushed her along to London Rehab. Carly signed in and knocked on her mom's door. It was 10:45, which was the usual time she arrived. A nurse took Ruth's vitals and tried to convince her to swallow her crushed pills. Carly's mom hated applesauce. They had to figure out a better way, Carly thought to herself.

"Hi, Mom!" Carly cheerfully exclaimed, dropping the overnight bag on a chair. She bent down and kissed her mom. Ruth smiled up at her as the nurse shoved the spoon in her mouth and gave her a glass of water to wash it down. In the past, her mother spat out the applesauce with the crushed pills mixed inside. Carly was thankful that today was not one of those days.

"Carly!" Carly was relieved that Ruth recognized her. Sometimes she looked at Carly with blank eyes. When Ruth looked at her absently, Carly's heart dropped to her feet, and apprehension emerged in her eyes. It always made her sad because she only visited once a week, and when the visits weren't good, it seemed like such a waste.

"How is she?" Carly asked the nurse before she hurried out of the room.

"Good. We switched her meds last night because she has been having difficulty sleeping. We'll know if it's a good fit by Friday. She's probably tired. Lately, she's been napping around one, which might be why she isn't sleeping well at night." Carly nodded, looking to her beautiful mom as the nurse left the room. It was hard watching her mother get old and sick. Carly used to feel resentful that her parents were so old when she was born, but Carly realized how short life can be and how quickly things can change.

"How are you feeling, Mom?" Carly asked.

"Good, good," her mother replied. Lately, the conversation was hard to maintain. Even though they didn't say much, Carly knew her mom was grateful for the company. Now and then, Ruth reached toward Carly and stroked her arm without saying a word.

"I brought your clothes." Carly unpacked and hung up the clothes in the bag and placed the dirty clothes in the overnight bag to wash at home. She also snuck a small unwrapped Hershey's chocolate bar and handed it to her mother. It was Ruth's favorite candy, and sneaking chocolate became somewhat of a tradition.

Carly wheeled Ruth outside into the warm, bright sunshine. They sat in silence and took in the environment. The warm sun, the birds flying above, the buzzing of bees, the lapping of the waves, and the quiet conversation of those around them put Carly at ease. Carly arranged lunch to be outside, and they ate in silence.

Although the conversation was limited, Carly shared what was going on in her life. Stories of her new houseguest, the cook-out, the newspaper assignment, and her shopping excursion to brighten up the carriage house monopolized the lunch conversation. She tried to take pictures on her phone often to help stir up some memories for her mom. She thought maybe seeing the carriage house would trigger a memory or seeing the most recent sunset would trigger a story about better days, but it never did. Her mom just smiled and nodded when Carly showed her pictures.

After lunch, Carly wheeled her mom back into her room for a nap. She looked tired. Carly placed a throw over her mom's shoulders, turned up the television, and kissed her on the cheek. "Bye, Mom. I will see you next week. Thanks for having lunch with me." Her mom smiled and turned her attention to the television. Carly grabbed the overnight back and headed to the ferry. Just another day in the life of caring for your elderly parents, she thought to herself.

* * *

The hot sun beat down on Joanie's back as she walked to her car. The humidity was stifling, and she found it difficult to breathe. She had so many thoughts running through her head. It was like her thoughts were competing with each other to gain her attention. They bumped into each other and ricocheted off her skull. She dug into her bag and pulled out the travel-sized bottle of Advil.

What was she going to do? Where was Mark? Should she continue working on her assignment? Should she be looking for other jobs? The number of unknowns overwhelmed Joanie, and she stood, paralyzed, unable to decide or process her options. Joanie texted Mark again and reviewed the message history. She sent seven text messages of increasing urgency over the past week, with no response. Joanie didn't want to go back to the island and didn't want to stay at home. If she stayed at home, she would sit on her couch alone, pretending to watch television, while running her mind off a cliff with all the what-ifs.

Joanie climbed into her car and threw her work bag onto the passenger seat. Instead of going home, Joanie decided to drive by Mark's house. If he was home, she was going to knock on his door and demand answers. If he weren't home, she would leave a note on his door begging for reciprocity.

Traffic was atrocious. Mark lived further into the city, which required special attention to all the merges, unfamiliar potholes, and random rotaries located in overcrowded towns and cities. Joanie wasn't usually brave enough to venture into the city during rush hour, but her body wasn't communicating with her brain, and all common sense had disappeared.

Joanie couldn't remember exactly where he lived, but she thought driving in the right direction would trigger the memory of how to get to his house. Perhaps muscle memory would kick in.

She delivered an article to his home one time in the past. He was livid with her that day because she almost eliminated the entire Lifestyle section. "How do you even explain that?" Mark asked. "Do you leave out a section and hope no one notices? Do you put in old articles and hope no one notices? Do you include sub-par work and hope no one notices"? He was red in the face, talking fast, and complaining that he would be up all night because it was his head on the chopping block.

Joanie felt terrible that day, but her grandmother had just died. She thought she deserved some sort of compassion, and she wasn't getting it from Mark. Maybe she should have told him she wasn't mentally able to handle all the juggling of work and home, or he should have known. Maybe this job wasn't meant for her.

As Joanie drove, her phone pinged. Frantically, and without taking her eyes off the road, she searched within her bag for her phone. Call me. It was from Mark. She pulled into the strip mall parking lot and called.

"Mark!" she exclaimed when he answered. "Where have you been?"

"I have been on the phone all day desperately trying to figure out what is going on! Sorry I didn't respond to your calls. I didn't want to talk until I had something to say. Can you talk now?" he asked.

"I was on my way over to your house. But I don't remember where you live," Joanie said sheepishly. "Do you want to grab a quick bite to eat? I am sitting in front of a coffee shop. There is a restaurant here if you want to grab some food. I am in Medford right now." Mark told her he would be there in ten minutes and would explain everything.

Joanie sat at a pub table facing the parking lot. The table was covered in shredded lettuce and drink rings from soda cups that perspired in the hot summer. She ordered a lemonade to buy some time. Her lemonade was chilled, sweet, and sour all at once. The cool liquid felt refreshing as she swallowed. Her stomach jumped into her chest as Mark climbed out of his car.

Mark erratically entered the restaurant and scooted into the bench across from her. "Hi," he said, wearing a crumpled white button-down shirt that appeared to be worn three times before today and not washed. He set a folder of papers on the table. Beads of sweat formed across his forehead, and his glasses slid down to the tip of his nose. He clumsily readjusted his glasses and wiped his forehead.

"Joanie. I am telling you, I had no idea. I woke up, like every other day, and turned on the news while I got dressed. I saw a snippet on the news. All it said was that they sold us. I was shocked. I spent the entire day calling Mr. Hill, the owner of Boston Tribune, trying to get a hold of anyone at headquarters in Chicago. After a lot of phone tag, voicemails, and messages, I finally got through." Mark stopped and waited, but no response came. He continued, "How has everyone been this week?"

"Well, you know ...nervous, afraid, and not very productive. I told them they need to have their articles in as usual, and we would make sure things went off without a hitch. I'm assuming we're going to be the headline on Sunday's front page?" Joanie waited for Mark to answer, but he fumbled on his phone, responding to an email. Joanie ignored his distraction and continued. "Everyone has a lot of questions. I have over one hundred emails from concerned employees with questions ranging from job security to healthcare to unused vacation time. So, tell me, what is going on?" Joanie asked assertively, staring directly into his eyes. She held his gaze until he responded.

"Well, it's true. The sale of the newspaper closed yesterday. Mr. Hill didn't want it to happen so fast, but once the news came out that we were down in our quarterly report and were losing money, Chicago made an offer he couldn't refuse. It's so funny that we talked about the potential crisis not even a month ago, and now here we are. No, not funny. It's ironic, sad, and shocking. By us being in Boston, it made sense for Chicago to try and broaden its scope. Now they are a media giant in Chicago with offices in Boston and LA."

Joanie sat quietly for a moment. "So, what's going to happen to us?" she asked.

Mark shrugged. "I don't know. It's too soon for any definitive information. I know that on August 15th, people from headquarters will be coming in, looking at our work space, finished products, and interviewing folks to keep their jobs. From what I gathered, September 1st will be the day we know for sure if we have a job or not."

Joanie smiled behind her anxiety. September 1st. That was less than two months away. In two more rent checks, her future would be decided with very little say from her.

Joanie stood up, told Mark she had to go and went home to lose herself in reality television while eating frozen pizza and forgetting that this was happening in her real life.

The next day, at the office, people kept to themselves. There wasn't the usual laughter or gossip floating over the cubicles. Joanie closed her eyes, and all she could hear was the clicking of keyboards. She wasn't sure if people were invested in their work and proving their worth or if they were hurriedly updating their resumes.

She printed out her article and put it with the other Lifestyle reports. She liked to keep hard copies, just in case something came up at home and she didn't have access to her computer. She sent everything to the editor to arrange for Sunday's paper.

Joanie packed up her bag and left for the day. It was time to head back to Carly's carriage house and figure out what she would do for the following article. August 1st was a few weeks away, and by then, her future may wither away.

Chapter 8

Carly flipped the bacon sizzling in the frying pan. She had three hot pots and pans on the stove—one for bacon, one for eggs, and one for pancakes. The coffee brewed, and the aroma filled the room. She closed her eyes, inhaled deeply, and then flipped and stirred. It was 7 am, and breakfast ran from 7:30-9:00 in the dining room. Today she had three of her four guest rooms full. Joanie returned late last night. Carly saw the taxi pull into the driveway at dusk. Joanie pulled out a small duffel bag and hurried into the carriage house.

Carly wasn't sure if Joanie would come for breakfast, but she knew it was always available. Carly was getting used to having a second person on the property, even if it was just a few days at a time. It was difficult for Carly not to think of Joanie as a guest because she had been serving guests for years. She often resisted the urge to enter the carriage house when Joanie wasn't there to clean the kitchen and change the sheets.

A few days before, Carly bumped into Matt at the grocery store, and he asked her when Joanie was returning. Carly looked at his tall frame, dark hair, and tired eyes. She thought of his life and their relationship and wondered how two single cousins, right around the same age, living in the same place, were practically strangers. Matt came by every few weeks, but he never stayed. They were connected, yet they didn't even know each other. She told Matt that Joanie came around on the weekends and would be back on Friday

53

or Saturday. He smiled and said, "Maybe I will see you around."

The tea kettle whistled, and Carly trotted back into the kitchen. She heard the guests congregate in the dining room as they helped themselves to the toast and juice station. Carly placed all the hot food in metal containers and finished setting up breakfast.

"Good morning!" she called as she strolled into the dining room. Six strangers sat at three different tables and greeted her with a mix of emotions. Some smiled, some buried their noses into a newspaper, and some continued to look out the window, commenting on the wildlife outside.

"Today, for breakfast, we have scrambled eggs, hash browns, pancakes with homemade syrup, and honey from the island. Coffee, tea, and juice are over here," Carly waved to her left. "Toast and pastries are over here," Carly pointed toward the table on her right, feeling like Vanna White. "Enjoy!" she exclaimed as she exited the dining room.

She sat at the kitchen table and picked up the paper. Block Island had a newsletter that came out monthly. It primarily contained classifieds, advertisements for seasonal businesses, and a calendar of festivals during the spring and early summer. Because her guests came from all over, Carly's inn received various newspapers daily, which cost quite a bit of money. Still, she felt that touching actual newspapers made her bed and breakfast experience more authentic.

The Boston Tribune was one of the papers delivered every Sunday. The front page had an article about The Boston Tribune sale. Wow, Carly thought to herself, I didn't expect to see that! She wondered if Joanie knew. She hadn't mentioned anything to her when they saw each other last week, but she did seem a little stressed. Joanie threw her messy hair into a bun and wore athletic shorts and running shoes. She told Carly she needed to investigate the island to get a feel for the culture. Carly didn't think anything of it at the time, but she wondered if running was her way of dealing with uncertainties.

The article said that a Chicago company bought Boston. The article mentioned that the transfer would occur on August 1st. Joanie looked at her calendar. August first was two weeks away. It said that they would notify employees by August 15th. Four weeks.

She flipped through the paper, pulled out all the store advertisements, and opened the Lifestyle Section. Joanie's article, Island Life, was on the front page, and this week's story was all about Carly. Joanie reviewed The Willowside Inn in such a positive light that Carly knew her business would soar.

Joanie wrote about the family history of The Willowside, the local ingredients used in her cooking, and the one-of-a-kind location. Joanie also mentioned the difficulty juggling a seasonal business, the loneliness of living on an island during the quiet months, and the community and camaraderie that other locals exhibited to support one another. Carly made a note to herself to ask Joanie about the two articles when she saw her later.

* * *

Joanie looked down at her phone. Thirty-five new emails and four voicemails in three hours. She haphazardly scanned through the notifications. Mark called once but didn't leave a voicemail. Her emails mainly were from co-workers panicking over their future. Joanie couldn't think straight, let alone deal with everyone else's questions and concerns. She turned her phone off, dropped it in her bag, and sat down in the patio chair outside the carriage house.

She closed her eyes and raised her face to the sun. The warm beams beat against her cheeks, and the cool breeze contradicted the warmth. She kept her eyes closed and allowed her mind to wander. She was annoyed at herself because thoughts of work were suffocating her. She knew she had to call people back eventually, but she decided today would not be the day. She felt the pressure to continue with her interviews but decided to wait another day. It was practically inevitable that she had to look for another job, but she decided to start next week.

The birds sang a tune from the high branches in the voluptuous trees next to her. She watched the flowers dance in the garden and saw the large, puffy clouds merge from one shape into the next. She listened to the music play faintly from the house across the street. She smelled the salt-infused air in the breeze. She closed her eyes and sat in silence, feeling satisfied with her loneliness.

She thought about the events that led her to this place. How did one small decision result in some dominoes falling into place, some falling out of place, and some remaining upright? She thought about where she wanted to be in a year, how little she enjoyed her work, and how little time she had to pursue her hobbies.

When she was a young girl, all she wanted was to be happy. She pictured her life like a storybook. Her dream included a house with a white picket fence, a garden, two kids, one dog, a handsome husband, and a job that gave her fulfillment. The job piece was never clear in her mind. She had no idea what she was doing in her dream. She only knew that it brought her joy, peace, and fulfillment. Her fantasy made her heart smile, while in reality, work filled her with boredom and anxiety. She imagined herself kneeling in the garden, retrieving beautiful round vegetables. Her straw hat, blue fitted gloves, and jean overalls were gently soiled with the Earth.

Her two children played in the yard with the dog and laughed gleefully as the dog ran over with the ball. Her children were never clear either, but she knew one was a boy and a girl. When she entered the home to cook dinner with fresh vegetables, her husband set the table and lit candles within the centerpiece on the table.

Joanie shook her head and looked around her reality. She lived alone in a dingy apartment. There was no man in her life, and there hadn't been one for years. She practically lived at the office and ate breakfast, lunch, and dinner behind her desk nine days out of ten. She spent her free time sitting in her car, crawling everywhere she needed to be or sitting in a jam-packed train trying not to breathe because people were either sneezing, coughing, or smelled of smoke and alcohol. There were no children, no real relationship with her family, no friends, and no husband. She smiled sadly to herself as she realized that her life was nothing how she dreamed it would be. There was so much lost potential.

"Knock-knock!" Carly called out as she walked toward the patio. Joanie squinted up at her through the rays of sunshine and smiled. "Can I sit down?"

Joanie gestured to the chair next to her, and Carly plopped down. "I didn't realize you were back! I brought you some leftover breakfast from this morning if you're hungry." She handed Joanie a plate filled with pancakes, a side bowl of syrup, and a large bowl of fresh fruit.

Joanie took the food and ate the strawberries with her fingers. "Thanks! I'm starving!" Joanie flashed her a genuine smile. "Sorry I didn't pop in yesterday. I have a lot on my mind," she said sadly.

Carly leaned forward and placed her chin in her cupped hands. "Yeah, about that..." she started and stopped. "I saw the articles this morning. Is it true that somebody bought the Tribune?" Joanie pursed her lips and nodded slowly. "What does that mean?" Carly asked. "I mean, what does that mean for you?"

Joanie shrugged her shoulders. She honestly didn't know. "I don't know, and I won't know until August 15th. The good thing is that I am kind of in a management position, so I hope they find value in my skills, but there is no guarantee they will want me, and there is no guarantee that I will want them. I have been there forever. I haven't been on a job interview in over fifteen years. I'm almost forty, Carly. I am too old to be job hunting. I never thought I would be in this position." She felt tears build up behind her eyes but refused to let the warm, salty liquid spill onto her cheeks.

Carly leaned across her chair and gave Joanie an awkward hug. Joanie remained sitting against the chair back and accepted the hug from Carly. "I read the article that you wrote about The Willowside," Carly said. "That was beautiful!"

Joanie smiled. "You're welcome. Thank you for being a great interviewee. It made my job that much easier."

After a few moments of silence, Carly said, "You know, you're welcome to stay here as long as you want. I like having you around."

Joanie didn't know what she wanted. She thought about how many failures occurred in her life and how she never fulfilled her dreams. She realized that they were never even attempted to be fulfilled. "I thought I would be there forever. Not because I love it, but because it's comfortable. I know my job, I know the people, and I know how to manage. The idea of applying for a new job or a new career is terrifying. What if I apply for something and I don't get it? What if I do get it, and then I realize that I hate it? Do you think security is more important than passion?" Joanie leaned forward and searched Carly's eyes for guidance.

"Well, what is your passion?" Carly asked.

"I don't know! I don't know if I have any passions! What if I am a passionless person who is never going to find happiness or her true calling?" Joanie leaned into her hands and wiped the tears away. They weren't tears of sadness but were tears of frustration and despair.

"Well..." Carly began. "I don't know you very well, so I certainly hope I'm not overstepping, but from one girl to the next, I think you deserve to be happy. And if that means you leave your job and try something totally out of character, I think you need to do it. What's worse than taking risks and failing is not taking risks and wondering for the rest of your life where your life would have been if you were just brave enough to follow your heart."

Joanie nodded as she swallowed back her tears. She felt misplaced and overwhelmed. She closed her eyes and let her senses calm her mind. A few minutes later, Joanie opened one eye and saw that Carly was still sitting next to her with her head back, taking in the warmth of the sun.

Later that day, Joanie reached out to Matt and asked if he would meet her near the police station. She needed Matt to give her a tour of where he worked so she could explain the intricacies of working on a small police force.

They agreed to meet the next day, right around lunch. Before leaving the carriage house, Joanie looked at herself in the mirror. Her red hair frizzed with the humidity, so she pulled it back into a low ponytail. Joanie wet her hands under the bathroom faucet and smoothed back all the tiny hairs sticking out around the curve of her face. She decided on a floral sundress but quickly discarded it because it felt too dressy. She changed into her favorite pair of jeans and a form-fitting white t-shirt. She threw on a couple of bright red wooden beads to give her bland outfit a pop of color and decorated her ears with silver hoops. The only makeup she wore was mascara and lip gloss, and she threw them both into her bag. It wasn't much, but she felt comfortable and confident. She ignored the nerves in her belly, grabbed her purse, and headed out the door.

Joanie arrived at the park first and sat down on a wooden bench facing the surf. A few swimmers braved the cool water and bobbed up and down with the waves. A little girl walked with a woman along the water, collecting what appeared to be rocks in a yellow plastic bucket. A man threw a frisbee to a golden retriever who raced up and down the sandy stretch. Even though it wasn't hot, there was still activity on the beach, and Joanie loved to watch people anonymously.

Across the grass, Joanie saw Matt. Her stomach alerted her before her brain processed his movement. She looked down at her feet, not understanding what her body was telling her. He wore blue jeans that hugged his butt, a black t-shirt, and a baseball hat, which shielded his eyes. She didn't know if he was looking at her, and she hoped he didn't realize she was watching him. She smiled brightly, just in case. Watching him without being detected caused her stomach to flutter and hop. She took a breath through her grinning mouth and slowly approached him, her hands in her pockets.

"Hi!" she called out. "Thank you for meeting with me!" He smiled at her with his white, straight teeth and full lips. "I, uh..." Joanie stammered. She didn't like talking to people in general, and now she had to speak to someone she found extremely attractive. "I, uh, was hoping I could ask you some more questions about work. I have to have another article by Thursday morning. I was hoping you could give me a tour of the station."

"Ah, I see. So, you're just using me to get ahead at work?" Matt smiled as he sat down on the bench. "And what do I get for helping you out, yet again?" She heard the flirtation behind his words and wanted to flirt back but didn't know how. All possible responses in her mind sounded flirtatious, but the consonants and vowels wouldn't form on her lips.

"Well...what would you like?" She bowed her head down and looked up at him through her lashes, hoping she sounded and looked desirable. Joanie felt empowerment fill her body, pushed her thoughts aside, and flirted back. She stared into his eyes and silently pleaded that she radiated control and confidence. "If you are lucky, you get me for dinner as a thank you."

It was like every movie she ever saw was taking over her body and words. Her mind was screaming, What are you doing? But her actions were in control. She couldn't stop the friskiness even if she tried. "Dinner. Tonight. And then, anything you need, I will say yes."

Matt looked deeply into her eyes, and Joanie saw the playfulness grow within the creases of his eyes. He held her gaze like it was magic. She tried to break away but struggled and found herself fumbling with the keychain in her hand.

"First, you show me what I want, and then you get what you want," Joanie watched his hair gently move in the breeze. His thick, dark hair was taunting and daring her fingers to comb through it. She wanted to feel his head, touch his hair, and kiss his forehead. She quickly shook her head, and the rational part of her brain kicked in. What was she doing? She was working and could not get caught up in a beautiful man she barely knew. She made a note to talk to Carly when she got back. "Are you ready to give me a tour?" Joanie jumped up from the bench, threw her bag over her shoulder, and started walking toward the police station.

Chapter 9

When Joanie returned to the carriage house, she saw Carly watering the garden bed directly in front of the inn. "Hey, Carly!" Joanie called out. She didn't want to startle her. Carly turned and gave Joanie a wave. "Hey, can I talk to you about something?" she sheepishly asked.

"Sure, what's up?"

"I wanted to talk to you about your cousin, Matt. What's his story?" Joanie didn't have time for small talk, so she jumped right to the point.

Carly furrowed her eyebrows. "What do you mean?"

"I mean," Joanie began, "is he dating anyone? Has he had a lot of girlfriends before? Does he have any kids?"

Carly laughed. "No, Joanie, he doesn't have a girlfriend, and he certainly doesn't have any kids. Well, none that I'm aware of, at least. If he has a girlfriend or kids, they certainly don't live here. He left Block Island after high school and came back a few years later. Ever since he came back, he's been single. It's not like there are many dating options on the island, and if he did have a girlfriend at one time or another, it would have gotten back to me. This place is small, and news travels fast. I think he works a lot and spends time at his parent's farm."

"Oh, does he live on the farm?" Joanie asked.

"Yes. They left it to him when they died. The inheritance paid the mortgage, so all he had to do was pay taxes. I don't think he wanted to stay, but free rent is free rent, and he didn't have any reason not to. I know the farm isn't producing anything, but the land sure is pretty. Why do you ask?" Carly questioned.

"He asked me out to dinner. Well, I mean, I asked him out to dinner. I don't know what got into me," Joanie felt the words tumble out of her mouth like a leaky faucet. "Tonight. I wanted to say no because I have to work, but the word yes came out of my mouth. I just wanted to make sure he wasn't a serial killer or the father of three," the words continued to cartwheel out. "And I have nothing to wear because I didn't pack anything dinner-worthy." She looked at Carly's designer clothes, manicured nails, and neat, highlighted hair. "Would you mind helping me?" she pleaded.

Carly smiled and nodded her head. The girls entered Carly's apartment and pulled open her closet door.

* * *

Carly sat at the kitchen table in her apartment and opened her computer. She had emails from the booking websites, and it seemed that the following vacancy wasn't until Labor Day. Reservations slowed down around Labor Day when kids went back to school, the weather chilled, and the ferries traveled less frequently.

Even though things slowed down, Carly still couldn't get away beyond her weekly trip to the mainland to care for Ruth. Carly tried not to resent her mother or other women, but it was hard when you felt trapped in a life you didn't choose.

Carly thought about the fall and what exactly it foreshadowed. No new faces littered the island, shops became dark, and the quiet nights would soon characterize her days. Winter was difficult to predict because although they didn't get a lot of snow, they sometimes got a lot of ice, rain, and wind. Carly knew that power outages lasted weeks before things were fully restored. That made it especially hard for her because she had to rely on cellular towers to manage the incoming appointments and reservations at the inn.

Carly pulled out her calendar and wrote down the new reservations. Even though she had no control of how busy the house was, it helped her plan her week to see how much prep time she needed to get the bedrooms ready for the newest visitors. It was important that their first impression of her was perfect and the bedrooms were clean and pristine. Anything less than a 4-star rating online could destroy her livelihood.

Carly dreamed about magically beaming herself to the coast of Maine. Often, when she went to sleep at night, she fell asleep to images of her past. When she was younger, she was full of love and life. She wouldn't think twice about dancing in the rain, going to the beach and searching for the perfect shell, dancing all night long at the cafe in town, or ordering a ten-pound lobster just because she could.

Living with John was tough because the money was inconsistent, but their fun was irreplaceable. They lived in a studio apartment in Portland and often ate rice and beans or whatever mistakes the restaurant made. John used to joke that he should call the restaurant and place a fake order, so they could eat the leftover food at home. Usually, the food she got to bring home was because the customer ordered a dish without mushrooms, and the cook wasn't paying attention, or the waitress wasn't clear in the order. It wasn't an easy time in her life, but she was young and in love and didn't care.

As Carly reflected on her life, she realized that those years were the most rewarding because Carly didn't have a plan. She could do what she wanted without getting approval from anyone but herself. John was never home during the summer because it was prime lobster season, so Carly tried to pick up double shifts to compensate for the slowness in winter. Winter was brutal because John was out of work, but they managed with the money squirreled away from the summer before. They enjoyed being together, and winters became her favorite season because she had John all to herself.

Carly closed her computer and looked at her calendar again. It didn't look like there would ever be a time when she could get away again. Carly wanted to run away and never look back. She wanted to go back to Maine, where she didn't know anyone, and no one cared if she stayed home, went out, or ran through the streets in celebration of her birthday. Suddenly the walls in the kitchen slowly closed in on her, and deep regret settled into her bones.

She didn't know what had gotten into her or why she was suddenly feeling so melancholy. It could have been because Joanie was on a date, or it could have been because her birthday was approaching. Her life was nothing like what she planned, and she started to wonder what her life may have been like if she told her mom no and stayed in Maine.

Carly reached for her computer again and signed into social media. Carly pulled up the search bar and typed John Nichols. There were eight John Nichols registered. Carly recognized her John Nichols immediately. She quickly clicked on his profile and scanned his wall. She saw pictures of him holding fish, sitting on a boat, sitting outside around a firepit, and drinking beer. None of the photographs gave Carly a clue as to what his relationship status was. She didn't want to contact him if he was married or had children, but she didn't see any sign on his profile saying yes.

Before she could stop herself, she clicked add friend. Then she clicked on Messenger and typed: Hi John. It's me, Carly. I was thinking of you tonight and hoped that you are doing well. She stopped. Was that it? There was so much she wanted to say but was afraid to open up and be vulnerable. She decided to wait until he responded before revealing too much of herself and hit the Enter key. That was that. Either he would respond, or he wouldn't, and either way, Carly would be okay with it. She closed her laptop, grabbed a beer, and watched a movie, obsessively checking her phone for a response.

* * *

Joanie dropped herself on her bed and stared at the ceiling. She wore a pair of tight black pants fitted to the ankle with black strappy sandals and a white blouse with a black camisole underneath. The light from her nightstand emitted a beige hue and caused shadows to dance on her ceiling as the cars drove by. She stayed like that for what felt like hours. She faintly listened to the radio that hummed in the kitchen, which she forgot to turn off before she left for dinner.

She sat up in bed and looked at her hands. At the end of the evening, Matt graciously grabbed her hand as they exited the restaurant. He told her he had a great evening and wanted to get together again. Matt looked handsome in his dark blue jeans and green polo shirt, which matched his eyes. He was cleanly shaven, which Joanie loved. Just seeing him as she walked toward him on the sidewalk was enough to get her belly flipping and her heart racing.

Conversation during dinner was more natural than she expected, especially with her nerves running in every direction. Matt took her out to a cute Italian restaurant with small bistro tables, candles, and white tablecloths. Joanie laughed to herself and prayed that she wouldn't drop red sauce all over Carly's clothes. Matt returned her smile and said he was a slob from all those years living alone and eating in the recliner in front of his television. He read her mind. At a different time, Joanie would have found that information to be a turn-off, but tonight she found it endearing.

They talked about a variety of topics, introduced mainly by Matt. Joanie didn't know how much personal information was adequate to give on a first date. She wanted to know everything about him but didn't want to appear nosey or desperate.

Matt led the conversation the entire night, but Joanie counter-questioned everything he asked. She learned that he wanted to be a police officer ever since he was a little boy. He always imagined himself in a big city where crime commonly occurred. He enjoyed working in Providence, but it was lonely, despite always being surrounded by people.

He had limited money during that time in his life. He worked fifty hours a week, lived in a closet-sized apartment in a bad neighborhood, and struggled with his girlfriend. He worked so much, all he wanted to do on his time off was sleep, and she didn't understand how or why she wasn't his number one priority. She took it personally and blamed their issues on his work schedule.

Matt's girlfriend, Sasha, was younger than he was and wanted a boyfriend who would be there and spoil her with gifts. Matt couldn't do that because he was working fifty hours a week and barely had enough money to pay the rent. He felt inadequate around her, and it was clear that she felt like he wasn't good enough for her either.

Their relationship quickly fizzled out, and Matt's rent was due. He rented month to month and decided to pack up and move home. He applied for all sorts of jobs on the island. His parents welcomed him with wide, open arms because they were disappointed when he left, but they always knew he would be back.

His parents took a trip to Florida to celebrate their wedding anniversary and drove because his mother feared flying. She flew once before, but then 9/11 happened, and she decided she would never fly again. She didn't want to put her life in the hands of a stranger. They rented a car and drove to Florida over three days.

During this time, Matt applied for a position on Block Island because rumor had it that Officer O'Connell was getting married to a woman from New York who had no desire to move to a tiny island. While Matt waited for Officer O'Connell to resign, he worked with Lucas and Logan at the fish market. It was an excellent opportunity to network with locals and tourists alike.

When his parents drove home from their beachside vacation, a tractor-trailer swerved into the left lane and smashed into his parent's small SUV. According to the police report, the driver fell asleep, and his parents were in the wrong place at the wrong time. There was nothing his dad could have done to avoid the collision, and that was it. They were gone.

"That was the story of why I left and why I came back." Matt took a sip of beer and waited for Joanie to respond.

Joanie didn't want to pry for more information.

After the waitress delivered their meals, Matt requested, "Tell me your story."

Joanie felt uncomfortable talking about herself because it seemed so mundane compared to what he had experienced. "Well, let's see," she started slowly. "I often wonder what my life would be like if I were born into another family. My life has been predictable, boring, and uninteresting. I have two parents, one sister and have worked at the same company for the last fifteen years. My family isn't close. I wouldn't consider my sister a friend, and I don't have any friends to speak of, except for Carly and work colleagues. I feel like there is so much more out there for me, but I don't know what it is or how to get there. And that is my boring life story." She giggled because the wine started to get to her head.

Joanie noted not to bring up Matt's parents again. It made her hands sweat.

As the alcohol started to flow through her veins, Joanie's muscles relaxed, her words formed easier, and her laughter increased. She felt amazing and stopped worrying if she was making too much or too little eye contact, laughing too much or too little, or if she said something stupid. By the end of the night, she loved the freedom of her words and the interest from Matt.

After dinner, they walked along the water and stared at the giant, bright, round, yellow moon. They searched for the man's face on the moon and described the shapes of the clouds as they rolled by slowly. Joanie saw an elephant riding a motorcycle, and Matt saw three balloons. The moonlight illuminated the waves lapping against the rocks. At that moment, Matt leaned over and kissed Joanie. It was a gentle kiss that lingered longer than it should have. Joanie stood on her tiptoes and leaned into him. She was yearning for more.

Matt pulled away and offered to walk her home. Joanie tried her best to hide her disappointment and smiled up at him. He asked if she wanted to see him again, and she grabbed his hand in confirmation.

Joanie thought about their night while sitting on her bed. Her head felt foggy, and her body felt hot. She touched her hand, her arm, and her lips. She slithered out of Carly's clothes and climbed into the shower. The heat from the water fogged the mirror and made it hard to breathe. Joanie climbed into bed wearing clean pajamas and dreamed of the night she had been dreaming about for years.

Chapter 10

T he following day, Carly groggily opened her laptop. Please no response. Please no response. Please no response, Carly silently chanted to herself. She thought about what she did and wondered if there was any way she could delete the message she sent the previous night. Her brain bounced around in hyperspeed and bounced from one idea to the next.

The last time she saw John was not a pleasant experience. She called him selfish for choosing Maine instead of her. She cried and begged him to stay. She sat in her car and screamed at the top of her lungs, banging her hands against the dashboard. She felt like she wasted time on a man who wasn't willing to be there for her when she needed him most. She deleted his phone number from her phone and deleted their text messages. When he said he wasn't willing to stay with her, she decided she was unwilling to keep trying, and the relationship quickly ended.

It ended cold turkey, and Carly got wrapped up in the details of running a bed and breakfast and managing her mother's health. She had so much to think about in her new life and old home that she couldn't think about John. That was where their story ended.

Looking back, Carly realized that she was the one who was being selfish for asking John to uproot his entire existence. Maybe the better discussion would have been if Carly wanted to go home. She was angry that she felt obligated and deflected her anger to John. She hated to admit when she was wrong, but she needed to apologize.

Carly quickly opened her social media and found nine new notifications from the night before and one message. Crap. Carly closed her eyes as she clicked on the message. She slowly opened one eye to see if the message was from him. It was.

Carly quickly opened both eyes and read the message while hearing the words in his voice. Hi, Carly. I haven't heard from you in a while. How is Block Island? Things up in Maine are going well. It's been a busy season so far. Do you need anything, or were you honestly just saying hi? He closed out the conversation with a smiley face emoji, possibly to lighten the mood. She quickly checked her notifications and found that he accepted her friend request.

Carly scanned his profile, looking for clues about his life. From what she could see, there was no girlfriend in the picture. Carly closed her laptop and sighed deeply. Life didn't stop, so she grabbed her mother's laundry and headed toward the ferry to ride back to the mainland. She decided to write back once she had a few hours to figure out what she wanted to say.

The weather was overcast, and the ferry was emptier than usual. Carly sat on the deck and felt the cool air and ocean mist blow across her face. Today, she dreaded this visit because she didn't get much sleep the night before, and these visits were always so draining.

Carly closed her eyes and pretended she was on a beach in Aruba. She imagined the blue-green water, the colorful coral reef, and the warm sun. She imagined the fruity drinks with little umbrellas, the colorful beach umbrellas protecting her skin, and the tan bodies on the beach. When she opened her eyes, she faced the streets of New London, awaiting her trek to the nursing home.

At Ruth's room, Ruth slept in an upright position, and a nurse checked her vitals. "Hi Martha," Carly said upon entering. Martha turned her head over her shoulder and made eye contact as she silently counted to herself. Carly dropped her bag on the pink chair next to the window.

"Hi Carly," Martha said as she picked up her chart.

"How is she doing?" Carly asked, nodding toward the bed. "Usually, she doesn't nap until after lunch."

"Your mom has been battling a temperature all night. She slept through breakfast and was agitated when we tried to give her medication. She's probably exhausted from fighting us." Martha reported.

"What do you think it is?"

"We don't know if it is just a virus or something more. We've been tracking her food intake at meals, and she seems to be coughing more frequently. We have her scheduled for an X-Ray to rule out pneumonia later today. Hopefully, it's just a virus."

Carly thought about the ferry she traveled on every week and wondered if she transferred germs from the handrails or seats to Ruth. No one called her with their concern, so Carly decided if they weren't overly worried, she wouldn't be distraught either. She made a mental note to grab hand sanitizer and keep it in her bag so she could sanitize her hands whenever she got off the boat.

That afternoon Carly sat in the pink chair overlooking the green field, waiting for her mother to wake up. Now and then, her eyes opened, and she asked for a drink. Carly and Ruth sat silently for most of the visit.

Carly looked at the black and white photos framed on Ruth's dresser. A photo of her mother and father holding hands on the dance floor on their wedding day was the largest frame. Curiosity, delight, and laughter twinkled in their eyes.

Another photo of her mother, father, and herself stared back at her. In the photo, Carly was about eight years old and squeezed between her parents on their loveseat, wearing their church clothes. A Christmas tree stood behind the loveseat, covered in lights, garland, and tinsel. Her parents loved to decorate for Christmas! The family of three had Christmas bows on their heads and tinsel in their hair. They appeared to laugh, with wide mouths and squinty eyes. Carly knew that her family was the most important thing her mother had, even if they didn't see eye to eye.

Ruth looked frail, with her bony cheekbones pushing against her skin and bruised arms exposed over the blankets. Carly never noticed before, but she appeared thinner and child-like. The neckline of her floral nightgown hung loosely around her bony shoulders. Her hair stuck up at all angles like a hand-drawn star a five-year-old would attempt for the first time.

Carly didn't want to leave her mother at the end of the day and worried that something terrible might happen. The nurse promised her that the x-ray would be done by five o'clock, and they would call with the results.

Carly reluctantly left because she had to get back to prep the inn for the next round of guests. After she returned home, she called the nursing home to check in on her mother. They reported that the doctor prescribed antibiotics for pneumonia. The speech therapist came in at dinner to do a swallowing evaluation, and Ruth tolerated a ground diet and thickened liquids without coughing. Carly knew that Ruth would fight the attendants at every meal if she couldn't eat the food she loved.

According to her mother, food was for enjoyment, not for survival. She spent most of her life cooking home-cooked meals for Carly's father and the guests at The Willowside. Not being able to eat her favorite foods was a huge adjustment when she first had her stroke. Eating a ground diet and drinking thickened liquids might kill her spirit and eventually kill her. Carly promised to return next week and requested a call if anything came up. She hung up the phone and slumped into the couch, thinking about the ups and downs of life.

She looked around her living quarters. The 450 square foot "apartment" still had pieces of her parents scattered throughout the rooms. The old teapot that her grandmother and mother used to drink from was still sitting on the counter. Carly didn't drink tea, yet the memory of her grandmother was strong when she looked at the teapot, and she couldn't bear to get rid of it. Ruth collected Hummels that sat on the mantle, covered in dust. Carly sat in the green armchair that her dad sat in every night to watch baseball. She found these relics comforting. They had become part of her because they were part of her history.

When her mom went into the nursing home, this apartment was a mess. Old newspapers and magazines that her dad read and saved cluttered the hallway. There were individual jars of spices, from who knows what year, lining the kitchen cabinets. The closets overflowed with clothes, bedsheets, blankets, and towels. Everything appeared worn and tattered and smelled like mildew.

After Carly's father passed away, her mother ran out of time during the day and couldn't quite keep the apartment up to her typical standards. When Ruth moved off the island, Carly spent the first month throwing out trash and knickknacks that her mother would never see again. It was an expensive endeavor because anything on the island was expensive, but Carly felt much better with minimal memories.

She hated feeling trapped. She was a grown, independent woman but felt like a ten-year-old girl trapped under her parent's rules. Usually, these feelings emerged when she thought about her life in Maine, and lately, she had been thinking about Maine a lot.

Sometimes she wondered what would have happened had she never returned to the island. She considered if she would be married, have kids, or what type of job she would have. It made her sad that she blew so much potential for her future. Why was she holding onto the inn? At first, she thought moving back would be temporary, just until her mother got back on her feet, but it had been years now. Ruth wasn't coming back.

Carly looked down at her calendar. Three more people were checking in on Friday. She made her grocery list for the weekend, folded the linens, restocked the brochures and activity center, and paid some bills. Carly sighed. Just another ordinary day in the life of an innkeeper.

* * *

Joanie felt a pit slowly form in her stomach as she approached her office. Her phone and email buzzed nonstop. Joanie tried to return messages, but it eventually overwhelmed her, so she turned her phone off. Her voicemail was full, and her email had an automated message saying she was out of the office.

Joanie took a deep breath, opened the door to the office, and trudged in. The lights sporadically turned on with her footsteps. The sunlight infiltrated through the window and generated most of the light in the room. It was eerily quiet, and there was no chatter, clicking of keys on the computer, or soft music playing in the background.

"Hey, Marley," Joanie called. "Is Mark here?" Marley nodded her head toward his office without responding. The door was closed, and the lights were off. It certainly didn't look like he was there. Joanie gently knocked on the door and waited. No response. She hit harder and waited. "Come in!" Mark's burly voice greeted her.

Mark sat behind his desk in a t-shirt and blue jeans. His hair was disheveled, his beard was sporadically growing in, and his under eyes were as dark as purple bruises. His laptop screen was open, and papers littered the desk and floor.

"What are you doing?" Joanie asked, eyeing all the paper on the floor.

A loud, bellowing laugh erupted from Mark like a volcano spewing lava. "Well, believe it or not, I am applying for a new job. Have you noticed that the entire office is empty?"

Joanie didn't respond.

"Yeah, it's been like that all week. Everyone decided that now is a great time to take all their built-up vacation days, which means no one is here. And if no one is here, no articles are getting written. And if there are no articles, there is no paper. And if there is no paper, there is no job." Mark spoke rapidly and cracked his knuckles above his keyboard. "So," he continued, "I am looking for another job. I have no idea what kind of job, but something. Because after this weekend, we have NOTHING," he yelled. "WE ALL WON'T HAVE A JOB!"

Joanie sat down in the chair opposite him. Her mind raced, and the sound of blood pumped through her ears. No articles. No paper. No job. She grabbed her cell phone and texted everyone in her department: EMERGENCY MEETING. TODAY. 3 PM AT THE OFFICE. She hit send, ran out of Mark's office to her desk, and wrote down every question she had for her staff. She needed to know everyone's intentions and thoughts about the buy-out if her job was on the chopping block.

The clock slowly ticked on. It was amazing how slowly time could pass when you were anticipating a defining moment in your life. This was it. Her make-or-break moment when she would either continue on the same path or bust free from her life, like a prison break. She heard the clock ticking, her pen clicking non-stop, and her knee banging against the underside of her desk like a metronome. She wasn't sure if anyone would show, but if they didn't, it was game over.

The green light on her radio sitting on the filing cabinet illuminated 12:56 pm. Joanie left the office to get some air. Even though the office was air-conditioned, she felt stifled. She felt her heart rate increase, her palms sweat, and her mind jump around. Joanie stepped outside and heard a blast of car engines, horns, birds, shuffling feet, and constant chatter. She found the nearest tree and slid down the trunk. She closed her eyes, breathed in, and counted to ten.

She pulled out her cell phone and searched for jobs within all the major yet local networks. Even if she took a pay cut, she would apply. Some money was better than no money, she decided. She found a listing for a team leader for one of the local papers, which could be a nice, easy transition.

The internet was slowly killing her income potential. What was she thinking, going into Journalism for college? She should have known that journalism would eventually die out with the introduction of the internet.

Joanie looked for customer service positions, which were plentiful. She didn't really want to answer calls of unhappy customers, but a job was a job, and she didn't have time to be picky. She saw that many of the hotels were hiring, some of which for management positions. She had no experience but was confident she could learn quickly, and discounted hotel rooms would be an added perk.

She refused to look into restaurants. Waitressing was all about communicating with people, which was not a strength for Joanie. Everyone had limitations, and Joanie knew hers fell along the line of restaurant management.

She looked at her watch. 1:38. She quickly got up from the tree and picked up a quick lunch. When she confronted her team, she needed stable blood sugar. She didn't want to crave chocolate when figuring out her future. By the time she got back to the office, it was after 2. Joanie prayed that people would come.

After forty minutes of pacing, eating chocolate, drinking coffee, checking her email, and working on her resume, Mikayla walked into the room. She wore baggy jeans, sneakers, a wrinkled top, and a ponytail. She had no intention of working today. She sat in the chair opposite Joanie and stated, "I'm here. Where is this meeting?"

"Conference room. I will be in one minute," Joanie gestured toward the door. Mikayla gathered her purse and left while Joanie grabbed a pen and a notebook. She followed Mikayla into the room and sat down at the head of the table. She waited for four other team members and told Mikayla they would wait until 3:15 before dismissing the meeting if no one showed.

At 3:13, Joanie's officemates surrounded her. She considered it a good amount since she called the meeting three hours prior. Mark didn't know that she was meeting with everyone, and she wanted to keep it that way. He left at lunch and never returned, so Joanie thought it was a good time. She knew that if Mark were in the office, no one would voice their honest thoughts. They would be more willing to tell her straight what their intentions were if the boss wasn't around.

"Hi, everyone!" Joanie smiled her most convincing smile that today was a regular day like any other. "I wanted to talk to you about the Lifestyle section of the paper. Does everyone have their topic for Sunday's printing?" She looked at them expectantly. Mikayla analyzed the cuticles on her already chipping fingernails. Danny flipped through the notebook he brought to the meeting. Susanna checked her phone, possibly for messages or email. Joanie felt her chest tighten and her throat close. She wanted to speak, but nothing happened.

She knew that if she waited long enough, the air in the room would become so uncomfortable, someone would burst open and answer her question. So, she waited. She sat down in her chair and leaned forward, pressing her chin into her closed fist. She breathed in for four seconds, held it for six, and exhaled for eight. She looked at her three officemates anxiously.

The lack of commitment within the atmosphere was slowly drowning

Joanie. She held on for as long as she could but anticipated panic. She did something she never wanted to do. She hated when her professors did it but suddenly understood why they called people out by name. "Susanna? Are you prepared for Sunday's paper?" Susanna snapped her head up like a jack in the box and hid her fingers in her lap.

"Actually…. yes and no," Susanna spoke slowly and deliberately. Joanie knew that if Susannah admitted to not being prepared, Mark could fire her. Without a new job in place, Susannah could be in a financial mess. "I have a first draft written on that new restaurant that opened, but I am waiting to interview the owner." Joanie slowly nodded.

"Let's try this a different way," Joanie started. She decided a different approach might get her the information she required. "Mark is not here, you guys. It's just us. Let me ask you, do you see yourself working here in five years?" Mikayla remained stone-faced, and the other two shook their heads, unsure of how to respond. "We have a lot of changes coming up. A lot of unknown, which can be scary. I get it, you guys, I do. I am right there with you, not knowing what will happen or if I will have enough money to pay my rent. How many of you expect to be here in one year?" Again, no hands went up. That was the answer Joanie needed. Her ship was sinking.

"Where is Mark?" Mikayla asked.

Joanie shrugged her shoulders. "This might sound strange coming from me," Joanie started, "but if any of you need a letter of recommendation, I will gladly write it. In the meantime, you still have a job here and are still getting a paycheck from us. Please put forth your best effort until the future of the paper gets straightened out. Please send me your articles by Friday night. I will see you tomorrow." Joanie gathered her notebook and pen and was the first to leave the conference room and office. She needed air and needed to figure out a solution quickly.

Joanie went to her apartment. It was hot like a sauna because she forgot to turn on the air conditioner before rushing out the door for work. Joanie dropped her bag next to the door, kicked off her shoes, and turned on the air. She knelt on the floor and leaned her face into the vents of the air conditioner. The loud, forceful breeze calmed her mind.

Joanie sat at the table and pulled out her laptop. She reviewed the article she wrote about Matt and what life was like being a policeman on Block Island. She started her article describing the police station and finished it with Matt's personal story about why he moved back. Joanie made a few edits and then saved the file. She checked her email for the other articles, but no one had submitted them yet. Next, she checked her phone for text messages regarding work, and she had one email from Susanna asking her for a letter of recommendation. Joanie knew she had to write it but was disappointed Susannah was jumping ship so quickly.

Joanie texted Susanna agreeing to the letter and did not ask any other questions. She then sent a group text to her staff, reviewing that she needed all articles by Friday night. Unfortunately, there was nothing she could do. She was heading back to Block Island tomorrow.

Every transition back to town meant unpacking, laundry and repacking. Joanie continued with her day, hoping that nothing else would come up. She looked forward to going back to Block Island and escape the chaos of real life.

Next, Joanie scheduled an interview with Lucas and Logan, the fishermen. She wrote down a list of questions to ask, cooked dinner and headed to bed with a reality TV program to help her escape from her life. She couldn't wait to get off that ferry and step foot on the beautiful, untouched island, where worries seemed small, and beauty was abundant.

Chapter 11

C arly tended to the garden and hummed along to 90's hip hop as she pulled weeds and watered. Her fingers moved to the beat of the songs as she dug, pruned, and pulled.

She wrote back to John another message that didn't give away too much information. She wasn't willing to show him her heart for fear of rejection again, but she did apologize for treating him so poorly. Carly told him about the inn, the weather, and a brief overview of the last five years.

Every time her phone dinged, she looked down, hoping it was him. Sometimes it was, and sometimes it wasn't, but today they had been writing back and forth like pen pals.

He told her that he thought of her often and only wanted her to be happy. He alluded to possibly seeing her when the summer season ended, and they both had free time. Carly knew that his statement was a polite gesture without any likelihood of actually occurring. She agreed and said it would be nice because that was the polite thing to say. She wasn't going to allow her heart to believe it could or would happen. Carly wouldn't be surprised if there was no more correspondence by the time summer was over. When things went well, bad karma was always right around the corner, waiting to jump.

Carly was thrilled that he wrote back, that he thought of her at all, and that she was still present in his life, no matter how minuscule that presence was.

So, she continued to hum, sing, and pull until the flower bed looked clean, orderly, and professional. All the while, Carly dreamed about the life she was yet to have.

Her birthday was in October, which was perfect because Block Island emptied out by then. Labor Day was the last busy weekend of the season, and September and October were used to take care of all the housekeeping from the summer business. Carly was not strong in math, money, or finances, so it took her twice as long to figure out if and by how much she made in profit.

Her parents never ran into a problem managing their money. Carly never remembered a time when money was tight, even during the Christmas season. Her father invested in the Stock Market but did so responsibly. If Carly invested, she would be viewed as reckless and maybe even blamed if the business went under and she had to file bankruptcy.

To get through the winter months, Carly kept the inn open, but it was never consistent business. If she did have a guest, it was usually for two nights or less, which meant that Carly was still trapped cooking, doing laundry, and being present in the house. She never got a break and never got to leave.

When she got back inside, she checked her phone and found one missed call and voice message. The number had a Connecticut area code, and Carly immediately thought of her mother. It had only been 48 hours. Nothing could have gone wrong, could it? She thought. The voicemail was Ruth's nursing supervisor, Sharon. "Hi Carly, this is Sharon calling. Your mother was admitted to the hospital early this morning. Despite the antibiotics, she still had a fever, and her blood pressure dropped, and she was having difficulty breathing. Please call at your earliest opportunity." The message clicked off. Carly stared at the phone, not quite sure if this was real or a joke.

She sat on the stool beside the kitchen peninsula and stared at the phone. She listened to the message again. Yes, Sharon said that she was in the hospital. Joanie felt a pit form in her throat, which prevented any sound from escaping. She felt tears filling behind her eyes and felt the pressure build until the tears exploded like a dam breaking. Suddenly the air became thick and dense and difficult to breathe. Carly ran outside and sat on the doorstep, sucking in the cool air and waiting for the dizziness to pass.

She was afraid to call the nursing home. Afraid to look at her phone. Afraid to hear the voicemail again. She knew she had to call back, but there was still so much to finish before the guests arrived. She had sheets to wash, shopping to do, and guests she had to greet. She didn't have time to call a hospital and listen to a nurse or doctor deliver too much information in a language she didn't understand.

She did what she always did when life got overwhelming. She pulled out her grandmother's tea kettle, her favorite mug, sugar, and a Lipton tea bag and proceeded to pour herself a cup of tea, despite the temperature steadily climbing past 80 degrees. Dad, I don't know if you are with mom or me, but I need you, Carly prayed. Could you stay with her? Hold her hand, whisper in her ear, and tell her to be strong. Carly raised the mug and cheered to no one in sight, imagining that her grandmother and her father were there to keep her company. Once Carly felt brave enough, she picked up her phone and hit "Call Back." They transferred the call to Sharon.

"Hi, Sharon," Carly's voice squeaked out. The tone and pitch of her voice surprised her, for it sounded much too high. She silently scolded herself for being weak. "It's Carly. I'm returning your call." She desperately wanted Sharon to tell her there was a mix-up. She wanted Sharon to say that it wasn't her mother, it was her roommate, and the new nurse on staff told her to call the wrong family.

"Carly, I am so sorry to share this news with you. Last night we continued to watch her fever. She went to bed easily, and she surprisingly took her medication well. Around midnight, her fever started to spike, so we gave her Tylenol. When we got her up this morning, she was dizzy and weak, but she was up. She barely touched her breakfast and needed full assistance to get dressed and use the bathroom. When the doctor arrived, he listened to her lungs, and we called an ambulance. Her breathing had gotten more labored throughout the evening, and her oxygen level was low but still at a safe level. This morning it had dropped. She has pneumonia. We were giving her antibiotics, but they weren't strong enough, and her body couldn't fight. She will probably be there for the next two days, and then she will return to us." Sharon's story spilled out of her mouth like a slow leaky tire. Carly listened, but she just wanted the story to end.

"Is it just pneumonia, or could it be something else as well?" Carly asked.

Sharon paused before responding. "Well," she started and then stopped. "They are monitoring her heart due to arrhythmia. She never had an issue with an irregular heartbeat, but sometimes the bacteria from pneumonia can travel to the heart and interfere with her heart's function."

Carly stood at the counter with a stooped posture. She watched the tears fall directly down from the crest of her cheek to the granite countertop. "Is it serious?" she whispered.

"It can be fatal. The nurses are monitoring her. If you have more questions, I suggest you come to the hospital and talk to the doctor." Sharon recommended.

Carly disconnected from the phone call, and the tears fell in loud, heavy sobs. She had to see her mother, but how? Three guests were scheduled to arrive. Carly's body felt numb and not her own. She had a job to do here. Life couldn't happen. She wasn't ready. She had no help and no opportunity to close down the inn for the weekend. Even if she could, she couldn't afford to lose the income.

Her mother was almost eighty-four years old. She wasn't a spring chicken, and her health was weakening. Carly knew the time in her life would come when her mother would need her, but she didn't expect it to be now, during the busy season when she needed to be on the island. Carly lay on the couch and stared at the ceiling. Her mind ran in circles about what to do next. How could she be in two places at once? She would ask Joanie, but Joanie wasn't due back until late tonight, and Carly didn't have that much time. She had to go immediately.

She called the only person she trusted, and she knew her mother would approve. Matt hung around enough at The Willowside as a kid to learn the basics. He knew that the beds needed linens, how to cook pancakes, and where everything was in the kitchen. She called Matt, hoping he wouldn't pick up, but he did.

"Matt. It's Carly," she quickly said as she ran around the house, stuffing random clothes into an overnight bag. "My mom is in the hospital with pneumonia, and something is wrong with her heart. I have to see her for a few days. Would you be able to stay at The Willowside for me? Please, I am begging you. I have no one else to ask."

There was silence on the other end. Carly froze in place as her heart sank into her stomach. "Please," she softly repeated.

"Carly, I can, but I have to work the overnight shift Saturday night and Sunday night," Matt said.

Crap. Think, think, think, Carly! Carly thought to herself. Of course, he works. He has a job! Carly felt stupid for allowing that information to float over her.

"Can you please stay tonight? I have to get to the hospital. If I have to come home tomorrow, I will." She didn't have time to think right now. She just had to go.

"Yes. I will be over in five minutes," Matt eventually responded.

"Thank you! I will have everything written down for what you need to check in the guests. They should arrive after three." Carly ran through her closet and bathroom one last time and continued to stuff random items into her bag. Then, finally, she went into the kitchen with a pad of paper and furiously scribbled down important information about check-in and meals. This was the first time she ever passed responsibility for The Willowside Inn to someone else. Carly prayed that when she got home, the house would still be standing.

Chapter 12

T he trek back to Block Island was long and dreary. Thick, dark clouds overpowered the blue skies. Raindrops wanted to fall, but the clouds hung on tightly. It left a moist feel to the air, and as the boat buzzed through the water, the chilly air refreshed Joanie's skin. She pulled strings on her sweatshirt and tightened her hood around her face to keep the wind out. She knew she should go into the cabin, where it was warm and dry, but the abuse from the ocean waves grounded her.

It was Friday. Deadline day. The day her future would become evident. If her team didn't pull through for her, her job was toast. She knew that they needed their job, but she also knew they were frustrated and disenfranchised by the lack of information they received throughout the past month. Joanie looked to the sky and stared at the clouds. She debated staying in Boston until tomorrow, but what was the point? Either they came through for her, or they didn't. She could do nothing from there or here, so she decided to continue back to Block Island. At least the atmosphere and people would keep her mind off her impending doom.

By the time Joanie got off the ferry, she had been traveling for almost five hours. She didn't sleep much the night before, and she struggled to keep her heavy eyes open. All she wanted to do was crawl into her bed and take a nap. Perhaps when she woke up, she would be feeling more hopeful and less anxious.

Joanie made her bed in the carriage house before she left for Boston. The puffy pillows surrounded the head of the bed, and the floral bedspread was smooth and wrinkle-free. Joanie fell face-first into the bed, kicked off her shoes, and curled into a ball under the top blanket. When she woke up, three hours had passed, and it was practically dinner time. Joanie usually did her shopping the day she returned, but stopping at the market was the last thing she wanted to do today. She glanced outside her kitchenette window and saw the light on at the inn.

Joanie pulled on her jeans and headed over to see if Carly had any dinner to share. She wanted to share her week with her for the sake of processing what had happened. Maybe Carly would have an idea about what to do if the team didn't send her their articles.

"Hello!" Joanie called out as she knocked twice on the back door. The back door entered into the sizeable farm-style kitchen, where Carly prepared breakfast every morning. No one came, so Joanie knocked again and then turned the doorknob. "Hello!" she called again into the open house. She poured herself a glass of water, sat at the kitchen table, and wrote a note explaining that she stopped by and wanted to talk.

Joanie heard a door from somewhere in the house close and humming that got increasingly louder. Matt walked in, wearing earbuds, navy blue slippers, form-fitting jeans, and an oversized sweatshirt. He carried a laundry basket and placed it on the kitchen table. Joanie smiled big and gave him a little wave. He pulled out his earbuds and said, "Hey! I didn't know you were here!" Joanie thought she saw a delightful surprise pass over his face, but she didn't want to read too much into him.

"I was hoping to grab a bite to eat with Carly. Is she here? What are you doing here? Your laundry?" She giggled at herself for asking so many questions and felt a blush creep up the back of her neck. Seeing him with a basket of laundry in his arms got her excited, and she blushed further at the unexpected feeling coursing through her veins. She felt a magnetic pull toward him and walked over, picking up the earbud off the counter and taking a listen.

Matt smiled back at her, flashing his straight, white teeth. "Actually, no, she's not here. There was a family emergency. She's back in Connecticut. Hopefully, it's only until tomorrow because I have to work tomorrow night. She needed me to stay here to greet the guests and make sure they were set up and fed in the morning," Matt explained. "Do you like my music taste?" he asked with a sexy lopsided grin.

"Yes, I do. I was obsessed with grunge in high school." Joanie handed him the earbuds and felt a bolt of electricity run up her arm and to her heart. "Do you need any help? I could use a distraction," Joanie indirectly requested.

"Right now? No help. I'm just folding laundry, but you're free to keep me company. Tomorrow morning though, I could probably use help. I haven't cooked for more than just myself since—it's been years. And the only breakfast food I know how to make is cereal and toast. I was debating about getting breakfast catered for tomorrow, but if you can help, that would be awesome!"

Joanie thought about it. Tomorrow morning, she would wake up to hopefully four emails with four articles ready to go. If she got the articles, she would help Matt with a pep in her step due to the level of relief. If the pieces did not come, would she want to be in the kitchen? She would cry in her bed and wallow in the fact that she was jobless, poor, and possibly homeless. If she cooked with Matt, she might not be the best company, but at least she wouldn't be thinking about her future.

"Yes!" Joanie cried, "That would be wonderful! I have to warn you, though. I make some mean bacon. As we say up North," she joked, "it is wicked good!"

"Thank you!" Matt grabbed her hands in his and kissed the top of her hand. "You have officially saved my life and possibly saved the guest experience for tomorrow. Are you hungry? I ordered pizza." Matt invited Joanie to stay, and Joanie again felt her heart beat out of her eardrums.

"That sounds delicious! I'm starving," Joanie said. That night she and Matt had an impromptu date, although they would never call it a date, and sat in the kitchen with pepperoni pizza, a few beers, and ice cream for dessert.

Joanie couldn't believe how quickly her day had changed. The entire evening with Matt, she did not worry about checking her email or messages. She also didn't tell him anything about work because she didn't want to drag him down and dampen the mood. Instead, she only told him the good stuff about her life. He listened intently, and she felt amazing.

At the end of the night, she gave him a tender kiss and said, "I will see you bright and early, sunshine," and strutted across the lawn to the carriage house. She felt his eyes examine her body as she walked away.

The following day, Joanie woke up with the sunrise. The birds chirped, the coffee brewed, and the smell of java filled the house. Joanie fell asleep and slept hard all night. She didn't recall having any dreams but did fall asleep thinking about Matt, their impromptu dinner, and imagined what breakfast would bring. Joanie pulled open the bureau drawers and searched for something comfortable yet sexy. Her choices were slim. She had a pair of jeans that hugged her body in all the right places, a pair of black yoga pants that accentuated her curves, and a pair of shorts that her mother would deem as acceptable hiking attire. Joanie pulled out the jeans and a form-fitting plaid button-down with a black camisole underneath.

She looked herself over and placed her red beaded necklace over her head. Perfect. Now for hair and makeup, she thought. Joanie usually wore her hair in a ponytail because it was quick, but she felt that a ponytail felt too tom-boyish and might send the wrong idea. Instead, she drenched her hair under the showerhead and squeezed a dollop of mousse onto the ends. It wasn't what she imagined, but it was certainly sexier than a ponytail. For makeup, all she had was lip gloss and mascara.

It was only 6:15 am, and the people staying at the guest house certainly weren't expecting someone to look like they were working for a cocktail party. She felt confident and comfortable as she walked toward the main house with a smile plastered across her face.

When she walked into the kitchen, Matt scurried around like a lost little boy. He didn't know the layout of the kitchen, and he also didn't know the first thing about cooking. "I am here to help!" Joanie announced as the door shut behind her.

"Great!" Matt said, "I have no idea where to start." He awkwardly approached her and touched her hair. "You look beautiful," he whispered. Joanie locked eyes with Matt. She couldn't break his trance. She had so much running through her head but couldn't get the words out. So instead, she smiled, leaned in, and hugged him.

"Good morning!" she responded. Heat rose up to her face as her inner voice chastised her for not returning the compliment.

"We need to make pancakes, sausage, bacon, toast, and scrambled eggs," Matt rattled off, reading the list Carly left. "What can I do, and what will you do?"

Joanie pulled out the pancake mix box and threw it towards him. The box crashed into his chest, and a cloud of mix puffed out the top of the box. Joanie giggled and tousled Matt's hair, shaking out the extra batter mix. Finally, she laughed and said, "I am so sorry! Here, you can mix the batter, and I will prepare the eggs. Let's throw the sausage and bacon on the stove now since it takes a while." Matt took a handful of dry mix and threw it towards her playfully with a smile. It coated Joanie's face, and they both laughed.

They worked in silence as the morning wore on, listening to the radio play one-hit-wonder hits from the 1980s. Joanie danced around the kitchen, quietly singing to herself and giving cooking hints to Matt. They made a good team, Joanie decided. Joanie did most of the cooking while Matt set the tables. People trickled in for breakfast. After breakfast, Matt and Joanie sat at the private dining table in the kitchen and ate together.

Joanie always struggled with making conversation, but she felt surprisingly comfortable with Matt. It was almost like they had known each other for years. Every time Matt looked at her from the corner of his eye, her stomach flipped and turned. Her hands grew clammy, and her breathing grew shallow. The feelings were too much for her to process or understand, so she clumsily got up from the table, cleared her plate, and told Matt she had to go home and get to work. He watched her leave, wondering what he said or did that upset her.

* * *

Ruth laid in the hospital bed, eyes closed, quietly breathing, taking her usual nap. Tubes exited her nose, and monitors beeped like the drumbeat to Carly's favorite song. The clock tick-tocked rhythmically, and her roommate listened to the television on a quiet volume.

Carly arrived yesterday evening and stayed at a hotel within walking distance to the hospital. Last night she met with the doctor, who told her that the antibiotics were not working as quickly as they would have liked. Ruth was in a state of congestive heart failure, which complicated the matter, but they were doing everything they could to get her back to the nursing home.

Carly's mind raced. Her shoulders tensed, and her head hung low. She rubbed her hands up and down her shirt, trying to remove all the sweat. As she left the hospital, she felt scared, worried, and anxious. Her world spun out of control. She laid in the bed at the hotel, with its thin, worn bedcover showing signs of cigarette burns and tears, feeling completely numb. She prayed she didn't bring home bed bugs, closed her eyes, and restlessly slept the night away.

She immediately came back to the hospital the following day, praying that there would be a change. But, instead, Carly sat in the chair directly across from her mother all morning and waited. She continued to sit as day turned to night. She didn't want to go home until Ruth left the hospital.

Carly called The Willowside to see how the morning breakfast went. She was nervous that Matt would somehow screw it up because he had zero experience in the hospitality field, but he was her only option.

"Hello, welcome to The Willowside!" a deep voice bellowed. She could hear in his voice that he was smiling.

"Hi, Matt! It's Carly. I wanted to call and see how your twenty-four hours went."

"Carly, hi! It went great! Last night Joanie popped over because she needed to talk to you, and she saw that I was in way over my head. She helped me figure out the morning and came over to help me cook." Carly heard music in the background. "I think," he continued, "the morning was a success. No one died of food poisoning, no one choked, and one person even asked for seconds. So how is your mom?" he interrupted his thoughts with concerns regarding why he was there in the first place.

"Well, not great. That's why I was calling. You have to work tonight, right? I'm going to cancel all the reservations for the week. I can't leave my mom." It killed her to say that because she needed the money, but she wouldn't focus or give the guests the experience they deserved if she didn't go back today. It would be a disaster.

Silence responded. "Carly, we killed it last night. Let me talk to Joanie. She is here for the next three days. Maybe she and I can figure out a schedule to keep the doors open for a few more days. That way, you don't lose as much money if you do have to cancel next week's reservations."

Carly sat for a moment, unsure of how to respond. She had never given up control of the inn since she took over a few years back. She never even had an employee because winters were so hard. "I can't pay you," she said bluntly.

"Carly, we're family! Think about it. Call me before my shift, let me know, and give your mom a hug and kiss from me," Matt said confidently.

Carly hung up the phone and continued to sit, staring at her mother. She couldn't believe this is where her life took her. She knew she would deal with the death of both parents eventually, but she wasn't even forty yet! Her mom should be healthy, cooking breakfast for the guests, gardening in the spring, and knitting in the winter. She should not be this sick this early on in Carly's life. Carly fought back the tears from sliding out the corner of her eye and stared out the window. The fear of being an orphan slowly crept into her, but she refused to let that fear swallow her whole.

The nurse walked in and smiled at Carly. "Just taking vitals," she said, seeing the concern across Carly's face.

"How is she?" Carly asked, rising from her chair and stepping forward.

The nurse took a few minutes to read the numbers and documents on her chart and then approached Carly. She motioned to the seat, and both women sat, side by side like Carly was about to receive the weekend gossip. "Her heart rate is down, her blood pressure is low, and her respiration is slower than we would like. The doctor is here doing his rounds. He will be in shortly if you want to wait. He might be able to answer your questions," she grimaced at Carly, not fully committed to smiling.

Carly sat for what felt like an eternity. The breakfast trays left, the lunch trays arrived, and no magical doctor appeared. Carly's brain shut down. She couldn't think about her mom, the Willowside, and certainly not about her return home. To pass the time waiting, she opened her phone. There was a message notification, and Carly felt her heart jump against her chest.

Hi Carly! I was thinking of you this morning. Do you ever come back to Maine to visit? I would love to see you.

Carly couldn't help but smile. This was her ray of sunshine during this overwise draining day. This message gave her hope that life would eventually get better. She quickly wrote back and sent it before she could proofread, edit, or change her mind.

Hi John! No, unfortunately, I haven't been back to Maine since I left. It's just too hard to leave the inn for more than a day. But, hopefully, soon, I will be back up there, eating fresh lobster on the shores of Portland. If that day ever comes, I will certainly let you know.

Carly waited a few moments to see if he would write back, but he hadn't seen her message yet. She slipped her phone back into her bag and looked at her mom. No change. Her eyes were still closed, and the monitors were still beeping.

Carly heard a rap on the door, and she quickly stood up from her chair. A man stuck out his hand and said, "Hi, I am Doctor Meyer. I have been overseeing your mother's case." Carly took his hand, introduced herself, and sat back down, waiting for any news.

"Your mother is 84 years old and has cognitive weaknesses. She was admitted for pneumonia but also had congestive heart failure. When she arrived, the pneumonia was in both lungs, her blood pressure was low, and her respiration was low. Your mother is very sick. We are doing everything we can, but because of her age, her recovery will be twice as long as a healthy young person, like yourself, would require. The antibiotic is working, but not nearly as quickly as we would have expected. She is allergic to the number one antibiotic used to treat pneumonia. She is fighting to get healthy, but I don't want to give you false hope, and I don't want to scare you. Your mother is very sick, and we are doing everything we can to get her healthy again."

The doctor stared into her eyes, waiting for a response or a reaction, but Carly had nothing to give. She stared at her mom, lying peacefully in the bed, and the tears started to fall.

The doctor slowly inched his way out of the room as if he was never there in the first place.

* * *

Joanie's eyes sprung open with a start, and she looked at the clock. It was a little after midnight, and a pestering push crept into her mind. She couldn't shake it and wondered what was nudging her.

She shot up in bed like a disengaged mousetrap. Shit shit shit, she thought. The paper flashed through her mind like lightning. She ran to her laptop and pulled up her email. She was supposed to make sure everything was ready for the printer yesterday! Joanie forgot about her deadline due to the distractions caused by Carly and Matt. She prayed that everything was waiting for her in her email box.

As of yesterday, she needed four more articles. One article sat in her email. It wasn't written well, contained grammatical errors, sentence fragments, and was utterly disorganized. One email said that Susanna quit and would not be continuing with the job. She apologized for not writing an article. She also had an email from Mark asking her where her section was, then a second email requesting a meeting first thing on Tuesday.

Joanie sat there, staring at the screen. Her eyes frantically scanned the emails, searching for any missing information that was overlooked. She did not understand the magnitude of what just happened.

Panic and chaos surrounded Joanie. Anger boiled up from her toes to her ears. Frustration threatened the tears to fall. What was she going to do? She had two articles. Two. Two out of five, which meant that she failed at rallying her team and leading the way.

Her section would be eliminated this week. She immediately emailed Mark apologizing for her lack of leadership. She agreed to meet with him on Tuesday morning, which meant that she had to leave tomorrow. Joanie knew she was getting fired. No more job meant no more money. Her thoughts started to spiral out of control.

If he fired her, how would she get another job? How would she pay her rent? She picked up the closest item she could find, which happened to be an ornate, pink teacup, and threw it at the wall. It shattered into pieces of all sizes, and the tears finally escaped down her cheeks like a waterfall. Joanie threw her cupped hand over her mouth and raised her eyebrows in shock. One minute the teacup sat on the mantel, and the next, it was smashed.

She couldn't fall back asleep and was up and out of bed by 4:30 am. Joanie watched the sunrise over the ocean. The rhythmic slap of the water against the rocks put her at peace and released some of her anxiety. She walked the coast until the rising sun beat down on her shoulders, and Joanie feared she got sunburned. The salt air filled her body with relief, and the quiet cleared her hazy mind.

Walking back to the carriage house, she saw Matt in the kitchen window. Joanie knocked on the door to see if he needed any help. She needed to keep busy to keep her upcoming termination out of her mind. "Hey Matt," Joanie called out as she opened the door.

"Oh, hi!" Matt exclaimed. "I am drowning in here. Please save me. The pancakes are burning, I don't have enough burners for the sausage and bacon, all the dishes are dirty, and I ran out of wheat bread."

Joanie giggled, "Okay, okay, let me help. We can do this!" She grabbed an apron and got to work. "Where is Carly? I thought she would be back by now," Joanie asked.

Matt hesitated before responding, "Her mother passed away last night, Joanie. I was supposed to be working this weekend, but because she needed help and we are family, I was able to take a few days off. Unfortunately, I have to go back to work Wednesday and am working seven days straight. Hopefully, that is enough time for Carly to return home. If not, we'll have to figure something out. Maybe close the inn for a week until things smooth over."

Joanie felt the tears piling behind her eyes, making it hard to see. She was a mess emotionally, and couldn't handle any more pain, even if it wasn't hers.

She blindly flipped the pancakes onto the plate and buttered the toast in silence. She gave Matt a tight hug and felt his body stiffen in her arms. Joanie questioned if his tight body was due to the unexpected embrace or the loss of his aunt. She hugged him a few seconds too long, squeezed his hands, and kissed his cheek. "It will be okay," she whispered.

They worked in silence for the rest of breakfast and served the guests with smiles on their faces. Then, as they were cleaning up, Matt asked, "Hey, I wanted to talk about yesterday. Why did you leave so suddenly?"

Joanie sighed. She didn't feel strong enough to have this conversation right now. But, seeing how her job and adventure on Block Island were likely over, she decided to be honest with him. "Matt, I like you. I enjoy spending time with you and learning about you, but I need to tell you something. My last serious boyfriend was when I was in college, and it didn't end well. I felt so good with you yesterday. It scared me. My feelings are unchartered territory, and it overwhelms me. So, I did what I always do when things get hard. I left to clear my head. I'm sorry if that hurt you."

Matt smiled at her. "I hope you don't take this the wrong way," he started, "but right now, we are friends who enjoy spending time together. I don't like labels, and I barely know you, but I want to know you more. If being friends leads to something more, then I think we should explore it. No pressure. Just friends," he added, "for now."

Joanie sighed loudly. "Well, unfortunately, I think I am getting fired, so I don't know how much more time we can spend together," Joanie said with a quiver. She had never been fired from a job and had been at this job for her entire career. Her life path was now entirely out of whack.

Matt placed his hands on her chin and cheeks and wiped the tears with his thumb. "Please don't cry. Please don't be sad," he whispered. He held her against his broad chest as she sobbed into his shirt pocket.

They spent the rest of the day together because Joanie didn't want to be alone with her thoughts. Matt was developing deep feelings for Joanie, even though he told her it was casual. They ate lunch together, walked the beach, and sat under the trees talking. Joanie felt sad leaving but knew she had to find a job quickly. So, for today, she tried her hardest to enjoy every moment of this beautiful island before having to go back to her broken reality.

Chapter 13

"Metal or wood?" the representative from the funeral home asked. Carly looked around the room, noticing the antique lamps that faintly produced a glow on the fancy, Victorian furniture. Carly internally criticized their choice of white cushions on the high back chairs and low-lying couch. White was a terrible color. It could never hide the tears and sorrow that were shed on a nightly basis when the building was open. Funeral homes were meant to provide comfort but only provided confusion and internal chaos, Carly thought.

The man looked at Carly, waiting for an answer. "You know, white is a terrible color for sad people," she sputtered.

"I'm sorry?" the man asked. Carly missed his name. She couldn't even remember if he had told her. Maybe he didn't. Perhaps he had a generic name, like Dan, or a sophisticated name, like Everett. Carly looked at his bushy eyebrows, slicked-back hair, and round glasses. He wore a pinstriped suit, square-toed shoes, and a narrow, striped tie, which somehow fit the decor of the funeral home. She wondered if the funeral homeowners demanded that Everett dress the part to sell the casket.

"The furniture," Carly started. "White doesn't hide anything. Black or grey would be much more fitting."

Everett cleared his throat. "I will let the owner know." He cleared his throat again. "Now, for the casket. Would you prefer wood? Or would you prefer metal?"

Carly didn't know what her mom wanted. She thought her mother would have been more organized for her final resting place, but dementia certainly interfered with her ability to get her thoughts down on paper. Carly was always so busy with the inn, and her mother seemed so healthy, it never seemed to be a priority to find out the details about her death wishes.

"I have ten grand for everything: the casket, the flowers, the reception, and the burial. I was hoping you could give me the nicest, most respectable casket you can give me for 5,000 dollars. The most I can pay for your funeral home and the casket is 8,000. I refuse to take out a line of credit to bury my mother. Honestly, I want to get this over with, so whatever you can do to help me NOT make decisions is perfect for me." Carly's voice cracked, and tears filled her eyes. She willed them away. She hoped she didn't sound noncommittal, but there were too many choices for a single night that would wrap itself up into eternity.

Everett cleared his throat again and flipped through the demonstration book. He opened the first page and gave her two options for the casket shape. Carly picked the elegant, curved rectangle over the blocky rectangle. Next, he turned the page and offered two options for fabric. Carly picked red because it was her mother's favorite color. Next, he turned the page and offered two options for the presentation of the body. Carly chose the cheaper option because her mother never owned a single lipstick. Ruth never saw sense in spending money to get her hair colored or nails done, even in her old age. They carried on in this manner until the back cover was closed over the contents and the casket and arrangements were complete.

Carly smiled at Everett and gave thanks for working with her requests. She pulled out her checkbook and paid a deposit for the wake like it was an event that everyone was dying to attend. Then, she burst out laughing at the irony of her thoughts.

"See you Friday," Everett said. He held open the door, so Carly could return home and unpack her mother's clothes.

The Willowside closed for the week due to a death in the family. Unfortunately, there was no vacancy this week, but Carly couldn't worry right now.

A funeral to-do list grew by the second. Call the relatives, find pictures, make a collage, pick out flowers, pick out mass cards and readings for the service, and pick out an outfit for the wake. Finally, she wrote it all down and told herself that it would get done.

Carly flipped through her mother's address book and searched for family members. Her mother didn't have any living siblings but nieces and nephews scattered throughout New England. She didn't even know who was family, friends, and previous guests at The Willowside Inn.

Carly flipped through Ruth's tattered Rolodex and started with who she knew. She called her cousins in Rhode Island, Massachusetts, and Maine and told them to tell everyone who may have known her mother or would want to say goodbye. She also asked them to forward the obituary to their families and mutual friends. The obituary was going into the local paper on Block Island and the paper for Southeastern Connecticut. Carly thought the nurses and CNA's who had gotten to know Ruth over the years would like to come as well.

Having her list of things to do was good because it forced her to set her emotions aside and work through the pain. Matt came over and helped sort through the many photo albums Carly had pulled up from the basement. He pulled candid snapshots that captured life as it was occurring.

Carly thought that her photo album would be full of selfies when she died, with fake surprise, fake happiness, and fake confusion littering the backdrop. The photos Carly took today lacked authenticity, with all the added filters and the ability to delete. Carly loved that the pictures Matt picked out were honest, raw, and exhilarating. The photos encompassed the many emotions of Ruth and were perfect for her celebration of life.

Ruth would be buried next to Peter after too many years apart. Knowing that they would be reunited, even if only in death, gave Carly comfort. Her mother was the highlight of her father's life. It was apparent in his smile, his eyes, and his stories. Although Carly's parents were older than most when she was growing up, she always recognized the love they had for each other, and when her father died, her mother's heart broke.

To celebrate her mother's life, Carly watched The Wizard of Oz. Every year, they enjoyed that movie together and even dressed up as Dorothy, Witch Glinda, and the Wizard for Halloween when Carly was six. She used her favorite stuffed animal, a black dog as Toto, and placed him in an old Easter basket.

Carly poured herself a glass of wine, cozied up on the couch, grabbed her mother's blanket from the nursing home, and fell into the Wonderful World of Oz, where everyone had a happy ending despite the internal conflict and controversies.

* * *

The silence pounded against Joanie's ears. Joanie stared at her lap. Her fingers intertwined into each other and squeezed until all her knuckles cracked. She looked at the clock, knowing that her meeting with Mark was supposed to start four minutes ago. She could feel the lump in her throat increase in size and threaten to cut off her airway. The air conditioner was not nearly strong enough, and the beads of sweat slowly saturated her hairline. She heard footsteps in the hallway, and her heart pounded against her breastplate.

Joanie looked over her shoulder and saw the doorknob turn and heard the hinges creak open. She made eye contact with Mark and tried to give him her most apologetic eyes. Instead, she pursed her lips in anticipation. She was sorry that her team didn't come through for her. She was sad that she forgot to send in her section and that she let him down. But, she was also praying for a miracle that maybe, just possibly, Mark would overlook her incompetence and give her another chance.

Mark nodded. "Joanie," he declared in greeting. Joanie gave him a weak smile. She wanted to yell out her apologies but bit her tongue, forcing herself to listen. She decided only to answer the questions asked because she knew she would have a hard time stopping. So much of her life depended on this conversation. She didn't want to look back in an hour, replaying every conversational turn and analyzing how the outcome could have changed had she just said something different. So instead, she waited.

Mark sat at his desk, placed his chin on his fisted hand, and said, "So, how is your summer assignment going?" His question dumbfounded Joanie, and her mouth dropped open. Was he serious? Was he sarcastic or snide? She couldn't read his facial expressions or tone of voice

"Um," Joanie began, "the assignment itself has been going well. The rallying of the troops within my department has been tough." She decided honesty was best at this point.

"Your first two articles were great. The last one, I never got to see. It seemed that the printer somehow forgot to include your article. Unfortunately, they forgot to include your entire section. Isn't that strange?" Mark passively pressed her for information. She buckled under the accusation that he never said. Her section was not printed because of her ineptitude. She was the reason why they received negative feedback from the public and why they might lose their jobs. It appeared to Joanie that it was going to happen sooner than later.

"Mark, I am so incredibly sorry. It was my fault, but there would have only been two out of five articles printed even if I had submitted the work. Most of the reporters for the Lifestyle section either didn't turn in their assignment or turned in crap full of grammatical errors and fluff. So, yes, it is my fault that the section was not printed, but you would have been disappointed either way."

Mark leaned back in his chair, stretching his legs out. He folded his hands and placed them on his now protruding belly. "Joanie, we have gotten more emails, social media posts, and negative reviews over the past two days than I recall ever getting. People want a refund because their paper was not complete. I'm getting pushback from the owners who are getting pushback from the new company. If there was ever a good time to screw up, this was not it." Mark rubbed his eyes with his thumb and forefinger. "Do you want an Advil?" he offered while popping the top.

Joanie quietly nodded and held out her hand. "What can I do to help the situation?"

Mark sat there quietly. "I am sorry, Joanie, but we have to let you go. Your assignment has officially been terminated."

Joanie sat there for twenty seconds, just staring at the clock on the wall. It had been four minutes since he walked in the door. A total of eight minutes and her job was gone. Poof! It popped like an overinflated balloon. What was she going to do? She didn't have a job, and she had no money. She couldn't even get a roommate because she was living in a one-bedroom apartment.

She quickly stood up and grabbed her bag more aggressively than she intended. She threw it over her shoulder, knocking over the stand-up lamp beside her. She held it before it crashed to the floor and choked back the tears that were sitting in the back of her throat. "Thank you for your time," she whispered.

"Whenever you need a letter of recommendation, please let me know!" Mark called out as Joanie calmly walked out the door.

She ran down the hall, ignoring all of her colleagues. Joanie avoided eye contact and focused on the tile floor at her feet. They knew what happened, and Joanie could feel the fear, regret, and sympathy permeate the air. She aggressively pushed open the stairwell door and ran as quickly as she could down the flight of stairs and out into the open air.

She didn't allow herself to cry until she curled up on her bed with the curtains drawn and the lights off. The sound of trucks accelerating and cars honking wafted through her open windows. No one except her parents could help her, and there was no way Joanie would go to them for help.

Joanie took the next two days to apply for jobs. She analyzed her bank account and realized she had approximately one month of savings to get her through, as long as she continued to eat pasta, cereal, and frozen vegetables for all meals of the day. She advertised online for a roommate and a job. Her lease was month to month, so if she found a place that needed a roommate, she could permanently terminate her lease and move into an 8X8 foot prison cell. It wasn't what she wanted, but if she wasn't able to pay her bills, would she have a choice?

She applied for retail positions, waitressing jobs, and call center positions. She assumed the skill level was minimal, and she would be automatically hired. She had no experience with any of those businesses but knew she could learn if needed. The problem was that she lived in a high-cost area, and the rent was astronomical.

She thought about applying for jobs all over the country and just starting over. Instead, she looked for a cheap place to live. It was time to look at life from a different perspective. Maybe if she ditched all her plans, whatever path she chose would be the right path to take.

Joanie knew that if she stayed home, didn't get dressed, watched tv all day, and kept all the lights off, depression and anxiety would take over. She had to stay busy, no matter how menial it felt, or else she would get trapped into the mundane cycle of feeling sorry for herself and feeling guilty for all she didn't do.

Friday morning, she woke up and knew that she couldn't stay home one more day. She had to go somewhere. She told herself that she would scamper back to her parents with her tail between her legs if nothing came up by the end of the month. Her parents weren't exactly encouraging with her life choices. They couldn't understand why she never had a serious relationship, why her maternal instinct to procreate never pushed her to marry, or why she wanted to live in a city. Joanie knew that going home would be subjecting herself to hearing about how her life could have been different had she just listened to them all those years ago. She didn't want to do it.

She mourned the loss of her job, her life, and her security. Anger was the first step in the grieving process, and Joanie was pissed. She couldn't believe that her team let her down. Yes, she forgot to send in what she had, but even if she had remembered, she probably still would have been fired for not sending in the entire section. She knew that Mark let her go to save himself from the same future, which made her blood boil. She was just a pawn in the game of corporate life, and she had no control of the outcome.

Joanie grabbed her duffle bag and threw in a few changes of clothes. She thought that maybe if she were near the ocean waves, clarity would transpire within herself. She hopped into her car and drove to the Port Judith Block Island Ferry. Being around nature and people who didn't know the state of her life might give her time to process, troubleshoot, and figure out what to do next. She had nothing else to do, right? No job and no commitments. It was time to stop the chaos within her life and grab hold of her future.

Chapter 14

C arly's kitchen overflowed with food. Fresh fruit platters, cheesecake, strawberry shortcake, and homemade cookies littered her countertops. Her refrigerator smelled of tuna casserole, lasagna, and spaghetti. Her sink overflowed with dirty dishes from neighbors and friends giving her food. They stayed to chat and left with a stomach full of hot tea or coffee. Her living room smelled like a funeral home, with arrangements and vases shoved into every corner. Carly looked around, and panic rose in her belly. She ran to the bathroom to vomit the chaos and despair within her.

When she stepped back into the living room, she saw Matt sitting quietly on the couch. "I came to help. What do you need?"

Carly felt sincere gratitude toward Matt and everything he had done for her over the past two weeks. She hugged him and cried into his shoulder. His argyle sweater smelled of wet wool. She pulled herself back, wiped her eyes, and said, "The wake starts at 4:30. We need to be there by 4:00. I have to take a shower. Would you mind doing something with these flowers and all this food? It's making me sick." Matt nodded and started gathering the vases.

"I'll bring these flowers over to the funeral home. I'll see you there at 4." Carly smiled, put her hands together like she was praying, and thanked him.

Around 3:30, she was in the kitchen distributing the last of the dirty dishes into the dishwasher. The door swung open, and Carly heard a familiar voice, "Hey Carly!" Carly turned and saw Joanie, scanning the state of the kitchen and the state of Carly. Carly was wearing a black A-line dress, black pumps, and black beaded jewelry. Joanie stood there, awkwardly, as she put two and two together.

Joanie dropped her eyes and slumped her shoulders, trying to blend into the wall behind her. She didn't realize there was a funeral happening this weekend. She chastised herself for being such a horrible friend. She wrapped herself in her drama, and she didn't think about what was happening here.

Joanie slowly walked toward Carly, unsure how to proceed. Should she hug her? Say sorry? Suddenly, Joanie stopped at the end of the countertop, "I am so sorry about your mother," she said genuinely.

Carly's eyes filled with tears again. It was a never-ending supply of tears that had been building since the last time she cried, almost a decade ago, when John returned to Maine, never to come back. Carly's shoulders slumped down, and she buried her chin into her chest, her shoulders silently heaving.

Joanie put her arms around her and held her for a few moments, wondering how much longer she had to stay in the kitchen. Joanie shushed into Carly's hair, waiting for the sobs to dissipate. Finally, Joanie pulled away from Carly, looked directly into her eyes, and said, "I need to go get dressed. Leave me the address, and I will meet you over there." No one had to know that Joanie completely forgot. It was dumb luck that she showed up on the right day, but at least her friend wouldn't feel so alone.

"Thank you," Carly said as she proceeded to write out the name of the funeral home.

That evening was a blur. Carly's mother lay in the coffin, wearing her favorite slacks and sweater. Carly dressed her in her wedding band, her great grandmother's pearls, and a bracelet Carly made as a kid that her mother never threw away. Carly found the bracelet fifteen years later when looking for her mom's diamond bracelet for her wedding. She asked Ruth about the homemade bracelet, and her mom said, "When I look at that, I think back to when you were a little girl, and I was your world." She said it with sadness in her voice, which made Carly sad. It was true. Carly had grown up, and they had grown apart.

All Carly wanted was to get away from her family and home, but fate interfered and brought her back. This bracelet left an impression on her mother and left her with happier thoughts, so Carly placed it around her mother's wrist for the wake and burial.

People from Connecticut showed up to pay their respects in large groups. First, a wave of CNAs walked through, and then a wave of nurses came around. Carly was the only person in the receiving line next to the casket because she was the only one left. She felt isolated and alone and completely out of place with no one to lean on in the receiving line. There were only so many "I am sorry" phrases she could hear in one night.

Her cousins from all over New England showed up also. Carly felt terrible that she had a bed and breakfast and refused to allow anyone to stay with her during this time of mourning. Entertaining guests and keeping the house clean while grieving the loss of her mother overwhelmed Carly. She didn't want anyone to see her break down in tears because random objects in the house reminded her of Ruth. Carly struggled to accept that she was now an orphan with no family.

At the end of the night, the funeral home was emptying out, and only a few family members remained. Joanie stood with Matt as he chatted with their cousins from Maine. Matt probably hadn't seen them in twenty years, but it appeared they were talking and laughing like old times.

Carly sat down in a black padded chair in front of the casket and stared at her mother. She looked so strange with pale, powdery skin, freshly colored hair, and wrinkled lips. Carly hated open caskets because they painted a fake picture of a person she loved. Carly knew that others wouldn't feel closure without saying goodbye unless they could see her body one last time.

"Is this seat taken?" a deep voice asked. Carly wiped her eyes and shook her head no. She continued to stare at the casket and sighed deeply. "I am so sorry for your loss," the voice continued.

Carly turned and saw the familiar, kind eyes, the rough hands, and the long legs. "John," she whispered.

"Hi," he whispered back, "I am so sorry to hear about your mother."

Carly couldn't take her eyes off him. "What are you doing here?" she asked. "How did you know?"

She couldn't take her eyes away from his beautiful face, still in shock that he arrived. He looked just as she remembered but older. There were more lines and gray hair, but Carly recognized him immediately and felt her heart swell with memories. She couldn't help but smile broadly, despite the sad occasion that found them together again.

"I bumped into your cousin Michael at the fish market. He asked if we had spoken recently, and I told him a little bit here and there. Then, he asked if I knew about your mom. When I said, 'no,' he told me what happened. I'm sorry, Carly."

Carly nodded. She looked over at Matt and Joanie chatting with Michael and his wife. Michael was much older than Carly, so they were never close as kids or adults. She forgot that Michael lived in Maine and didn't ever think that he knew John. But, of course, they worked in the same type of industry, and Maine is relatively small, so it now made sense that they would bump into each other.

"I would have told you," Carly responded, "but I was so overwhelmed with how quickly she passed and how much I had to do to get ready for her services, I completely forgot. Thank you for coming."

John looked the same but older and wiser. His salt and pepper beard and fine wrinkles around his eyes aged him gracefully. He seemed heavier and fuller since the last time they saw each other. Nevertheless, he looked more confident and comfortable in his skin. Carly had a sudden urge to wrap her arms around him and feel his warmth emanate into her body.

They sat there, chatting like old times about Maine, Carly's current life, John's current life, and old memories. It felt normal and comforting to talk about something other than death and loss.

Eventually, the funeral home emptied, and all that remained were Matt, Joanie, John, and Carly. Michael and his wife left to grab dinner and told John they would meet him back at the inn. Not Carly's inn, but an inn solely used for people traveling for funerals. The inn was adjacent to the funeral home and was currently filled with Carly's long-lost family, whom she didn't remember or recognize.

Matt recognized John as Carly's ex-boyfriend but couldn't recall the details. Finally, he whispered into Joanie's ear, and they excused themselves. Matt leaned into Carly and said, "Call me if you need anything." Suddenly, he needed to protect her emotions.

Carly invited John back to her house to catch up on the last decade. Brain fog settled around Carly, and she felt like she was watching a movie of her life. She needed a mental break from the turmoil that jostled her, and John was the best distraction. His kindness and familiarity were all Carly required to make it through the night.

Chapter 15

Joanie rolled over and looked around the room. The bright sunlight diffused gently through the curtains, and her clothes piled on the floor. Next to her lay a man, his eyes closed, his hair ruffled, and his lean arms outstretched over his head. Joanie wondered what he was dreaming about and if he was dreaming about her.

The previous twenty-four hours were a whirlwind that she hadn't processed yet. The shock from losing her job dismantled her sense of stability. Then, seeing the abundance of food in Carly's kitchen made her realize just how much she cared for Carly. Her evening with Matt was out of character, but Joanie decided that her whole life may have been a charade until that point.

She would never have returned to a man's home in her previous life, especially a man she didn't know. Carly shared snippets of information about his leaving and returning to the island, and Matt shared snippets of information about his career and his family. Other than that, Joanie knew nothing.

She looked at her watch. The funeral services started in three hours, and Matt was a pallbearer. They had to get moving. Joanie quietly climbed out of bed and retrieved Matt's T-shirt, given to her as an oversized nightshirt. She quietly walked out of the bedroom, through the living room, and into the kitchen for necessary coffee.

As the coffee brewed, Joanie checked out her surroundings, looking for signs of a secret that would bring her back to reality. Could she find signs of a wife, an ex-wife, a girlfriend, or a kid? Instead, everything looked like what you would picture from a bachelor pad. The old sofa with uneven, well-used cushions sat in front of a television. Joanie recognized the nightstand holding up the television from her parent's living room during the 1990s. A two-person pub table and a fridge full of beer sat in the blank kitchen.

Joanie decided this place looked like it belonged to a lonely single man, not a man who may have a woman or child over for Sunday night dinner.

Joanie went back to Matt's bed, with black coffee in an oversized mug, and placed it on his bedside table. She gently shook his shoulder and whispered, "Morning, sunshine. Funeral services start in three hours. Time to get up." Matt moaned and rolled to face her. He smiled at her with his eyes still closed. "Morning, beautiful," he said in a raspy voice.

Joanie leaned down and kissed him on the forehead. "Coffee?" she asked, handing him his cup. He sat up in bed, took a sip from the mug, and grinned his lopsided grin that Joanie loved. "I need to get back so I can get ready. Would you mind driving me?"

Matt nodded, stretched, and grabbed his keys. He pulled on the black t-shirt that Joanie tossed on the floor the night before. She felt herself blush and was grateful for the dim light that hid her nervousness.

"I like your place!" she called through the bathroom door. "I thought Carly said you lived at your parent's old house." Joanie looked around at the small renovated barn.

Matt spat into the sink and turned the water on to wash away the toothpaste. "I did. This house we are in now was the barn at one point. It was too painful for me to be in my parents' home, so I took the money they gave me and renovated this place. It's not much, but I would rather be here with my stuff than in my parent's old house." He stepped out of the bathroom, and Joanie smelled his cologne emanating toward her like a magnet. She shivered in delight.

"Who lives in your parent's house now?" Joanie asked.

"I rent it out to a couple from Rhode Island. They work remotely and have a thing for fishing. When I came back, I had all the furniture removed and started new. The house I grew up in doesn't look like the house now, but I still couldn't bear to stay in there. The couple living there has been there a year or two. I think they're happy. I don't bother them, and they don't bother me. So, I have this little cottage with no one to worry about besides me. It's great."

Joanie felt her heart sink at hearing that he liked being alone. She fought the feeling but couldn't help but hear disappointment knocking on her heart. She hoped she didn't regret last night.

Matt drove her home. Even as they talked about the services and the memorial, Joanie couldn't help but feel giddiness and desire fill her belly. Despite the circumstances, she had more excitement these past twenty-four hours than she had in years. Joanie still couldn't believe she allowed herself to sleep at a man's house that she didn't even know. It was entirely out of character, but she felt a confident, beautiful woman emerge and overpower the awkward, insecure woman she had gotten used to throughout her life.

Joanie experienced a whirlwind of activity and emotion over the past few days. She experienced happiness, fatigue, anxiety, frustration, fear, sadness, and anger like an archer who took aim at her heart but occasionally missed. She kept her drama to herself because she didn't want to interfere with Carly's problems. It had been a few days since she sat down with Mark, and her world flipped on its lid. That moment felt like a lifetime ago.

Seeing Carly at the wake in such pain made her heart hurt. Finally, Joanie realized that Carly was more than a roommate or a landlord. She was a friend and the only friend Joanie had. That realization made her miss her sister even more, especially during this chaotic time in her life.

Joanie had no direction. She had no idea what tomorrow was going to bring, let alone next month or next year. Instead of feeling sorry for herself, she decided to feel free. Sure, she was broke, had an apartment she couldn't afford, and no job, but she was free to start over. Joanie wasn't sure where this newfound attitude and knowledge came from, but she decided to embrace it. Maybe it was because she felt her heart-melting whenever she was with Matt. Perhaps it was because she never wanted to be with someone, but she was getting older, and she found her mind continuously wondering about Matt and what memories they could share.

When she got back to the carriage house, she immediately called her sister. Jackie was never the person Joanie wanted to share her life with, but this confident and assertive Joanie called her sister.

Jackie's phone rang three times. Joanie expected it to go to voicemail, but Jackie picked up, slightly out of breath. "Hey, Joanie!" Jackie gasped into the phone.

"Hey. Are you okay? Did I wake you?" Joanie looked at her watch. Whoops. 7:30 am on a Saturday was way too early.

"Nah, I was just exercising. Is everything okay? I decided to get up early this morning and go for a run on the beach. It's beautiful today!"

Joanie looked out the living room window and noticed the blue sky and the magenta and lavender flowers in front of the house. The salt air traveled with the breeze, and the birds chirped in the trees between the carriage house and the main inn. It certainly was a beautiful day! "Yeah, yeah, everything is fine. I wanted to talk to you about something."

"Let me guess!" Jackie started. "Mom and dad are coming for a surprise visit," she giggled. "Or, you got a dog! Or you have a boyfriend!" Jackie was full of energy this morning, Joanie thought.

"Well…kind of. Do you want the good news or the bad news?" Joanie asked.

"Oh shit. There's bad news? I am going to go with the bad news first," Jackie said without skipping a beat. Joanie imagined her jogging on the beach, kicking sand behind her while speaking to Joanie on speakerphone.

"Yeah. I got fired." Joanie said definitively, not letting her bad news bring her down.

"You what?!" Jackie's voice elevated an octave as she screeched into the phone. It was evident that Jackie stopped mid-stride.

"Yeah, I screwed up. But it wasn't entirely my fault. A bigger company bought us. I'm sure you saw it on the news. We had until August 1st to prove ourselves to the new company. Otherwise, we would be let go. Well, my team under me jumped ship without telling me and just didn't turn in their articles. So, when everything was due, there was kind of an emergency here, on Block Island, and I forgot to turn in what I had, and the paper printed without our section," Joanie babbled.

"Wow!" Jackie exclaimed.

"Yeah, so even though no one did their work, I took the hit for everyone because I didn't turn in the section on time." Joanie paused, expecting a reaction, but nothing came. "I got fired," she continued.

Joanie heard Jackie fumbling with the phone but didn't respond. Joanie imagined Jackie transitioning from stopping to jogging. "Shit, Joanie, what are you going to do?"

"I have no idea! At first, I was upset because I thought it was unfair that I got in trouble even though no one did the work, but I kind of feel relieved. Like, this is an opportunity to find me. Recreate me and figure out what I want for my life, now that I am almost forty, kidless, and husbandless."

"Yeah, you don't sound sad about it. Do Mom and Dad know?" Jackie asked.

"No! And you can't tell them. At least not until I have a plan. Promise me, Jackie." Suddenly, Joanie's voice became stern. She remembered when they were kids, and Jackie saw her sneaking out of the house to meet up with some friends after her curfew. Jackie manipulated Joanie into driving her around town for a month at the snap of her fingers, or else she threatened to tell her parents. If her parents found out, they would have grounded Joanie from seeing her friends on the weekends, so Joanie agreed to be Jackie's chauffeur. It got to be too much, and Joanie eventually came clean to her parents. She told them what Jackie did, which was punishment enough, so neither girl got in trouble; Joanie for sneaking out or Jackie for being manipulative.

Joanie never trusted her sister again, and she learned that when she sneaked around her parents, she also had to sneak around Jackie.

"Yeah, yeah, your secret is safe with me. But they are coming for Thanksgiving, so you better have it straightened out by then. You know I can't lie to their face." Jackie said.

"Promise. Give me a month. I'll have a plan. Now, are you ready for the good news?" Joanie asked with a grin on her face.

"Well, you just got fired. Anything would be good news compared to that." Jackie exhaled into the phone. Joanie guessed she was cooling down from her vigorous exercise routine.

"I met a guy!" Joanie shrieked into the phone. She felt like she was in 7th grade again. She wasn't sure if she should tell anyone because it was so new, and there was a chance that Matt didn't feel the same way she was feeling.

Jackie shrieked into the phone with her. "Tell me, tell me, tell me!" It sounded like she was jumping up and down.

Joanie told her how they met, how they took care of the inn together, how they spent time on the beach and at his house, and how wonderful he made her feel. Then, finally, she told her that she needed to spend some time on the island to figure out her future. She and Carly had agreed until the end of August, and Joanie was praying that the offer still stood. That deadline gave her a few weeks to figure out her next move.

Joanie promised Jackie that she would ask Carly if she and Chris could come up for a weekend to spend time with her. Life was so unpredictable. Despite their past, Joanie decided she needed her sister.

* * *

The funeral was an absolute blur. Carly spent the entire ceremony with tears streaming down her face and sobs escaping from her lips. She felt so alone and isolated, sitting in the front pew of the church with aunts, uncles, and cousins she hadn't seen in over two decades.

When her parents bought the inn, they became a slave to Block Island, and Carly became a slave by default. Carly spent Christmas, Thanksgiving, and holidays alone because her family lived so far away.

Carly sat next to Matt, watching the priest's lips move but not hearing or comprehending a word. Her brain kept jumping around, like someone trying to tune in a radio station, but every time the signal cleared, it became fuzzy again. Memories from her childhood, her dad's funeral, and the nursing home all collided within her brain, fighting for her attention. Eventually, her brain numbed, and the memories subsided.

People that she had never met and never even heard of before hugged her awkwardly and softly. Nursing home staff, relatives, and previous guests who eventually became her parents' friends gave their condolences.

After the service, they traveled to the cemetery to lay Ruth next to Peter. Carly hadn't been to her father's headstone in years, and she mentally apologized for being such a terrible daughter. However, she felt comforted knowing that her mother was finally back with her father.

She felt a hand on the small of her back and turned to see John, standing behind her in a long, black trench coat. Carly smiled. She knew this was all he had brought to wear, and he was trying to look his best, but he looked silly standing in such a heavy outer garment in the middle of August. It wasn't even raining. Carly leaned into his broad shoulders and wrapped her arms tightly around his torso without saying a word. "Thank you," she whispered, looking up into his eyes. "I need you."

He stood by her side for the remainder of the burial and allowed her to lean on him when feeling weak, alone, confused, and sad. They had a lot to talk about but now was not the place.

Carly felt at ease next to him. His warm body erased the numbness within her, and his strength gave her the energy to remain upright. "Please don't leave me," Carly said. "I need you here. With me." John nodded and stayed by her side for the rest of the day.

At the reception afterward, a crowd of about forty people stayed. The reception was at The Willowside Inn because that was most affordable and appropriate since Carly's parents dedicated so much of their life to that place. Fortunately, the townspeople came together and dropped off potluck items throughout the morning, so food was plentiful. The weather held out, and the sun remained shining.

Carly saw one dragonfly land on the railing of the porch where she was sitting. It sat for about half a minute, just resting and looking at her. Carly believed it was her mom coming to visit. "I love you, Mom," Carly whispered to the dragonfly. After her words floated on a breeze, the dragonfly sailed away, and Carly watched until it disappeared in the distance.

She felt more comfortable and at ease at The Willowside. This was where she grew up. All she wanted was for people to leave, a bottle of wine to drink alone. She fantasized about sleeping the night away until the pain subsided. She yearned to forget that this was her life.

Joanie, Matt, and John stayed the entire day, which turned into evening, which turned into night. Finally, all the other guests slowly dissipated, leaving to catch the last ferry back to the mainland, heading home or heading to the inn next to the funeral home. The four of them sat outside on the open farmer's porch, looking into the fields. Lightning bugs sporadically put on a light show for them to enjoy. The warm evening air swaddled Carly in a blanket.

"Carly, do you remember trying to catch lightning bugs when we were kids?" Matt asked, staring into the night.

Carly smiled. "I don't remember catching them. I remember you terrorizing me with them."

"Wait a minute.... tell me the story!" John chided.

Matt laughed and pulled Joanie close to him. "I was five years older than Carly, so when she was seven, I was twelve. Our parents would have dinner together a few times a month, and when it was warm, we would eat outside. I was a horrible cousin and thought it would be funny to scare Carly. So, I captured all the lightning bugs I could find and trapped them in a jar. I told Carly that if the bugs lit up, it meant that they were ghosts trying to enter our world to take over our soul."

"Yeah!" Carly interrupted, "And of course I didn't believe him, and then he unscrewed to cap and only had his hand blocking the opening! Then, he threw them on me!" Carly laughed and shook her head in disbelief at the memory. "You were so mean!"

Joanie poked Matt in his side. "That is so mean!"

John pulled Carly close and hugged her from behind.

"Yeah, it was mean. I was a mean kid. What can I say? I got in so much trouble for doing that to you! Your parents and my parents took me inside and scolded me for being so cruel. And then they made me write you an apology saying everything I said was a lie."

Carly laughed. "You are the reason why I don't like camping! Too many

114

bugs that want to take over my soul."

They sat outside talking about life, death, childhood, and adulthood. Eventually, the three friends left Carly alone to think, grieve, or process. Carly realized that she was thirty-nine years old and officially an orphan. Those words seemed so harsh and unkind for someone so young. No mom, dad, brothers or sisters, husband, boyfriend, or kids. There was officially no one left whose job was to look out for her.

The feelings of loneliness and isolation wrapped themselves around her and squeezed her tight. She pulled her legs up into her chest on the chair and wrapped her arms around them. The numbness subsided, and the tears fell. Carly wished things were different. She was too young to be alone.

She took a sip of wine and continued to stare into the darkness. Her life had been a series of decisions made to make her parents happy, and now they were gone. As Carly looked back on her choices, she knew that she shouldn't have bent and accommodated their needs. Instead, she sacrificed her own life for their dream. Now she was running a bed and breakfast that she didn't even want. The feelings of anger and resentment crashed into the isolation, and loneliness and hatred filled her soul. She felt like so many opportunities were wasted to follow her dreams or live the life she intended.

Carly looked around and realized how much of the inn was for her parents and how little was for her. Sadness and resentment crashed into her anger and absorbed it. She cried not for her mom but the lost opportunity of her past and her future. Carly couldn't handle the mess of emotions within herself anymore. She took another gulp of wine and stumbled into the house to distract herself from her feelings.

Chapter 16

T he day after the funeral, Joanie sauntered into the Inn to check on Carly. They weren't expecting any guests until the following weekend to allow Carly time to organize herself and the piles and mountains of paperwork her mother left her. "Hello?" Joanie called out through the kitchen door.

"Hey! I'm in here," Carly called from the dining room. Joanie walked in to find piles of papers on every table. Carly was sitting facing the front window staring out into the yard with a hot, piping coffee mug in her hand. She took a sip and didn't move as she continued, "What do you think happens when people die?"

Joanie sat down next to her but didn't want to get too close for fear of making Carly uncomfortable. Carly didn't even acknowledge the movement across the room. "Um. I don't know. I believe that good people go to heaven, and I assume your mom was good. So, she is probably in heaven. I have no reason to believe otherwise. What do you think?"

Carly sat there in silence, watching the bumblebees travel from flower to flower. "I don't know," she whispered. She wiped away a tear that fell onto her cheek. "Do you think she is with my dad?"

"Absolutely!" Joanie quickly responded. "I do believe that when a man and woman love each other and give their lives to each other, they are together in life and death. And you were the third part of their heart, so you will one day be with them too."

Carly looked down at her lap, and her shoulders rose and fell rhythmically. "I hope so. I hope my mom in heaven is who my mom was the day they got married. I hope she's healthy. My dad missed her. I know it."

They watched another dragonfly flutter next to the window as if paralyzed by hope and sadness. Joanie and Carly sat in silence until the dragonfly disappeared into the branches of a nearby tree. Carly wiped her eyes and returned her gaze to her coffee. Suddenly her stomach turned, and she placed the mug on the glass table.

"Are you okay?" Joanie asked, touching Carly's arm. Carly looked over at Joanie. "I mean, I know you aren't okay. Your mom just died, but how are you holding up? Do you need help with anything?" Joanie scanned the room, assessing the various piles of paper.

"I've been up all night. Every time I closed my eyes, memories from my childhood crashed into me. One time, my mom taught me how to make my great-grandmother's chocolate chip cookies. Another time, my mom took me ice skating in secret because my dad was afraid that I would break my ankle. After mom took me, she bribed me with ice cream not to tell my dad. Another time, I got a horrible haircut, and my mom felt so bad, she went out and got the same haircut so we could look terrible together." Carly giggled, remembering how ridiculous they both looked. "I couldn't sleep last night."

"Your mom sounds like a beautiful person. She raised you, and you are a beautiful person too. You were lucky to have her," Joanie soothed.

Carly cried again. "I never acted gratefully. I hated that my parents were so much older than my friend's parents. I hated that they could have been my grandparents. I hated that I was stuck at this inn most of my childhood and missed out on fun activities because they were too busy taking care of guests. Yes, my mom was a beautiful person, but I was so ungrateful for her love. I was resentful that I didn't have a brother or sister because I was all alone. I hated being alone and feeling like an afterthought."

Joanie passed Carly a tissue and rubbed her arm. She felt slightly awkward, not really knowing Carly and not ever knowing her mom.

"But none of that matters," Joanie guessed. "Your mom and dad knew you loved them. Trust me, none of us had perfect childhoods, but it sounds like your mom tried to make it special when she could. She wouldn't have done those things if she didn't love you. You were her world," Joanie guessed again.

Carly nodded at her reflection in the window. "Thank you for listening." The conversation ended, and Joanie felt relieved because she didn't know what to say next. Finally, after a few moments, Joanie asked about the paper mountains littered around the room.

"Oh, you know, documents from the nursing home, insurance bills, birth certificate, passport, will, old bank statements. Who knows what else?"

"Do you need any help going through it?" Joanie asked. "I'm happy to help."

Carly shook her head, "It's going to take me a while, but I can get everything done and situated before the guests arrive next week." She continued to sit, staring out the window.

Joanie made her some fresh hot coffee and breakfast while Carly sat staring out the window like a statue. Then, Joanie ran to the grocery store to stock up on healthy food that would keep her going through the week. She dumped all the desserts and casseroles that sat in the fridge for days.

Carly continued to sit and stare until the sunset and the lightning bugs came out. Then she went to bed.

* * *

The following day, Carly woke up with the sun shining through her window. The sunbeams warmed her soul and motivated her to get out of bed and take a shower. She was so grateful for all Joanie did yesterday. It seemed to be the little things that completely overwhelmed her and paralyzed her from being active, organized, and in control. She recalled sitting, thinking, and processing.

Separating all those papers was enough for one day, and maybe today, she would tackle one or two piles. She was thankful that Joanie let her sit without judging or encouraging her to get up before she was ready.

After a hot, steamy shower, Carly threw on her sweats and a t-shirt before going downstairs. She technically got dressed, which was progress. She smelled coffee and bacon as she approached the landing of the staircase. Carly immediately thought Joanie was in the kitchen cooking food to get her body nourished.

Instead of Joanie, she saw John, facing the stove with his back to her, wearing her favorite apron, flipping bacon and sausage. Carly muttered a noise in her bewilderment, and John turned around with a smile on his face. "Good morning! I hope you're hungry!"

"Hi. How did you get in here?" Carly asked, crossing her arms over her braless chest.

"Many moons ago, you gave me a key. I've been holding onto it for years, never really convinced that I would ever see you again. I knew you would be sleeping, so I thought I would surprise you."

Carly walked over and gave him a stiff hug. She felt happy and confused to see him. She didn't know who they were to each other. Narrowed eyes and a smirk crossed her face because he let himself in without her knowing. She grabbed her sweatshirt from the couch and threw it over her shirt. Instantly she felt better.

"So, how long will you be in town?" Carly asked awkwardly, pulling her tangled hair into a ponytail.

John looked at her for just enough seconds to make her shift her weight from one leg to the other. She clasped her hands in front of her, quickly crossed her arms, put her hands on her hips, and then sat down to calm her anxious limbs.

"I have to head back tomorrow," John said. "I wish it could be longer, but you know how crazy lobster season can get."

John poured her a cup of coffee and asked if she still liked half and half with two sugar cubes. Carly laughed, flattered that he remembered.

She nodded and replied, "Only two sugar cubes and one teaspoon half and half. I wouldn't want to throw the proportions off."

When Carly and John lived together in Maine, they drank beer at night and coffee during the day. They were broke and couldn't afford to purchase coffee from an actual coffee shop, so they spent an entire day trying different coffee, sweeteners, and dairy products to find THE perfect cup of coffee. Carly found that sugar cubes were a better measurement than loose sugar, and it tasted perfect every time she tossed in two sugar cubes.

"Yeah, I thought it was kind of funny that you had sugar cubes in your cabinet, and I immediately thought of our coffee days," John said as he plopped two sugar cubes into her mug. Carly smiled, feeling nostalgic as the taste of coffee made by John hit her taste buds.

"Thank you," she smiled. "This is perfect."

She took another sip and thought about their tiny apartment in Portland overlooking the harbor. She felt content and satisfied as she sipped her coffee and ate breakfast that she didn't have to make for once. "I know you have to go tomorrow, but you are always welcome to come back as long as you would like. It would be nice to catch up after all these years," Carly said with a smile.

Carly and John spent the day together. He told her that his job was to make her feel better and ease her mind from the looming responsibility of going through her mother's estate. He didn't say that in quite so many words exactly, but Carly inferred his message. She was grateful for the companionship during this tedious and burdensome task.

"Thank you, John," Carly said, looking up at him, squinting her eyes because of the sun. The shadow of his six-foot frame towered over her 5-foot 3-inch shadow, and the two shadows mingled until they were one indecipherable shape. John leaned down and embraced her, wrapping his long arms around her torso.

"You're welcome," he whispered through her messy hair into her ear.

Carly pulled away and looked intently into his eyes. "I'm serious. When I was at my absolute lowest that night, having you there made the night a little more bearable. I had no idea you were coming, and I want you to know that I appreciate it. After everything I did to you, I didn't deserve to have you here." Carly heard her voice quiver and felt the peach pit grow in her throat.

John leaned down and tenderly kissed her lips. Carly wasn't ready for it, and her heart leaped into her throat. Her lips tingled. She pulled away and stared into his almond-shaped eyes. Her eyes traveled to the contour of his face, the shape of his lips, and back up to his eyes. She searched for something. Maybe it was honesty, or perhaps it was forgiveness, she wasn't sure.

After a few moments, his eyes showed fear and remorse and then confusion. Carly placed her hands along the back of his head and played with his hair. She pulled him into her and kissed him hard. Her heart exploded, and the tears fell from her eyes. She pulled away, wrapped him into a tight hug, and sobbed into his shoulder.

After a few moments, John pulled away and asked if she was okay.

Carly nodded. "When you left me, you broke my heart. I didn't understand how my requests were unfair to you. I don't think I ever allowed myself to grieve because I was so angry. I just picked up the broken pieces, stuffed them deep into my pocket, and never took them out again. I learned how to live with a broken heart. Then, when I kissed you, my feelings went crazy inside my body. Everything I felt toward you—the good, the bad, the great, and the ugly came crashing together. It completely overwhelmed me. I'm sorry." Carly looked down at her hands, curled together, hanging at her thighs, too ashamed to look at John. She was terrified to see the outcome of being so truthful.

John grabbed her hands, raised them to his lips, and tenderly kissed them. "I'm sorry," he whispered.

With that, Carly turned away from him and quietly led him up to her bedroom.

* * *

Joanie called Matt to ask if he could go for a walk down at the beach. Matt had two more days off for bereavement before having to head back to work. They met near the park bench where they had lunch the day of the newspaper interview. Joanie arrived first, holding two iced coffees. She wore her favorite jeans and a white tank top. The island had done her well so far this summer, and her skin had a warm glow to her otherwise pasty skin.

"Hey, beautiful!" a deep voice bellowed from her left. She turned to see Matt walking toward her wearing loose jeans that hung around his hips, black flip flops, and a black t-shirt that advertised a local bar. Joanie noticed that his hair was tousled and damp, and she wondered if he had just gotten out of the shower.

Joanie stood to greet him, and he gave her a gentle peck on the lips.

"Hi," she said, looking up to meet his eyes, smiling brightly. "I have to talk to you about something."

Concern flashed over his face, and she grabbed his hands and pulled him down to the bench next to her. She wrapped her fingers through his and covered the top of his hand with her other hand. She stayed like that for a few moments, trying to figure out how best to break the news that she was jobless, scared, and alone.

"I got fired," she exclaimed. No matter how many people she told or how many times she said it, she still felt the same level of shame cover her body. She looked down in embarrassment. At first, she felt angry and shocked that Mark fired her! But now, she was just embarrassed. She had been there fifteen years and was part of their family and then discarded like a bag of trash.

"I'm so sorry!" Matt said. "What are you going to do?"

Joanie felt tears form behind her eyes and didn't understand why. The thought of having no idea where her future was going terrified her. Fears related to disappointment, parent approval, and financial stability drove her emotions. Her biggest fear was that her life had peaked, and this was the best it would be.

Instead of answering Matt, Joanie leaned into his shoulder before he could see her tears and cried silently. She felt so stupid for losing control of herself.

Matt pulled her away from him and wiped her tears from her cheekbone with his thumb. "Shhh. It's going to be okay. You're going to be okay."

Joanie took a deep breath to compose herself. "I am so sorry. I don't know why I am crying," she said between giggles. "I feel so stupid. I know I'll be okay, but I don't know where to go from here. I feel like my life is sitting at a four-way intersection, and the light is stuck on red. All the cars behind me are beeping, and I'm afraid that if I run it, a police officer will pull me over and ticket me for doing the wrong thing."

Matt pulled out his badge and replied, "I promise, I will never pull you over for sitting at a red light."

Joanie giggled because her analogy didn't make any sense, but she hoped Matt understood what she meant. Hell, Joanie didn't even understand her feelings yet; it was evident that she couldn't articulate them properly.

"No, seriously," Matt responded, "you take as long as you need to figure it out. There is no harm in pausing your life to figure out your next move. It happens all the time in chess. Think of how long someone can sit before making a move in that game. And the reason why? Because every move has a reaction that can either help or harm them. There is nothing wrong with pausing. Are you heading back to Boston?" There was a glimmer of hope in his question.

"Not yet. I am staying at the carriage house until the end of the month. If I go back, I will fall back into the hustle and bustle of life. I'll probably decide what to do before I am ready. So, I am here for a few more weeks. I still have to figure out what to do about my apartment because I can't pay my rent if I am not getting paid. And I can't tell my parents. They will say I told you so, and I refuse to let that happen. Maybe I can find a job helping out somewhere to get some extra cash. I don't know. With everything happening with Carly's mom, I haven't spoken to her yet, but I will." Everything poured out of her mouth like a rainstorm. Matt had no answers for Joanie because, ultimately, she needed to seek out the answers herself. He cared for Joanie, so he listened.

They spent the afternoon talking about her job, her qualifications, her experiences, and her dreams. They didn't come to any conclusions, but Matt promised to ask around and see if she could help out somewhere on the island. She froze in a moment of uncertainty, but like life, things could change instantly.

Constant thoughts swirled in her brain, and it made her dizzy. That night she knocked on Carly's door to see if she wanted to eat dinner together. The kitchen door was ajar, so Joanie let herself in after knocking three times on the door loudly. "Carly? Are you home?" Joanie called through the doorway.

Carly walked into the kitchen wearing tight jeans, a cute button-down blouse, and black flats. Her neat hair and glowing face portrayed confidence and contentment.

"Joanie! Hey! How are you?" Carly responded with a smile.

Joanie struggled to recognize Carly. The despondent girl from yesterday who only moved to use the bathroom was now flaunting around the kitchen like a leprechaun who found the pot of gold at the end of the rainbow.

"Wow! You look amazing! Did I interrupt? It looks like you are going out on the town!"

Carly continued to smile; her lips curved up toward her cheekbones. "Oh, no! I had a great day today, hanging out with John, and I feel so much better than yesterday! I think all I needed was a hot shower and a good night's sleep." Carly sauntered over to the fridge and poured herself a tall glass of orange juice. "Do you want some?" She raised the orange juice.

Joanie shook her head. She looked into the dining room and saw the numerous piles untouched. Carly pulled herself together, despite the stress waiting for her in the other room. She seemed so upbeat at this moment; Joanie knew that this was the perfect time to break the news about her life.

She cleared her throat and turned toward Carly. "Can I talk to you about something? It's something that has been on my mind for the past few days." Joanie sat down at the kitchen table and patted the seat next to her. "Last week, I was fired."

Carly immediately sat next to her.

This was the third time Joanie told the story, and with every retelling, it felt more and more like it wasn't happening to her. Everything spilled out, but this time it was in the correct chronological order and void of emotion. "So," Joanie finished, "if you know of anyone who is looking for some extra help, please keep me in mind. In the meantime, I will be applying for jobs back in Boston. I might be here until the end of August, or I might leave earlier, depending on what happens with the job situation."

Carly reached over and gave Joanie a big hug. "Hang in there," she said, squeezing Joanie's forearm. "It will get better."

124

Carly comforted Joanie when Joanie comforted Carly the night before.

Carly's phone buzzed, and she said, "Hey, I'm sorry to cut this short. I'm meeting John for a drink. Can we catch up tomorrow?"

A moment later, Joanie sat alone in the kitchen, wondering how Carly transitioned from depressed mourner to giddy dater in a matter of minutes. It happened just as fast as Joanie having a job on Tuesday at 9 am and being jobless by 9:30.

Life was like a tornado. By the time the siren sounds, it might be touching down on your house while your neighbor's house is untouched and standing. You just never know what life will throw at you, Joanie thought.

Chapter 17

"I don't understand," Carly said to Bob Dryer, her father's attorney. She was holding a piece of paper with multisyllabic words and acronyms that she couldn't read, let alone understand. The entire document was mumbo-jumbo, and Carly needed Bob to translate.

"Your mother left her entire estate to you. Her money, her savings, her assets, and The Willowside Inn. She left you everything but did state that she wants The Willowside Inn to remain in the family for future generations," Bob said.

"Wait, what? How will she know if it stays in the family? I don't have any kids, and she is dead." Carly said flatly.

"Well, yes. That is correct. It seems that the person who drafted the will knew the legal complexities of that as well. Obviously, in your will, you can break that statement, but your mother intended for it to go to you, debt-free."

Carly sat there, anger fuming within her. She continued to feel trapped within her parent's expectations. She hadn't thought about selling The Willowside any time soon, but now that the option to sell was off the table, she felt defeated and frustrated.

"And what happens if I end up selling, for whatever reason? Maybe I need the money, or maybe I want to move, or maybe I need a change? What happens then?" Carly asked quickly.

"Well, if you sell, the proceeds from the sale will be divided up among all the small businesses on Block Island. Your mother and father worked their lives away to make the inn a success, and your mother wants to pay it forward to other struggling businesses. It's right here," Bob said, pointing to the disclosure. "Unfortunately, because Block Island is so small, the bank, the law office, the real estate offices, and the Town Clerk are all aware of her wishes. I don't know how you would get away with selling and keeping the money for yourself. This is a small island, and everyone knows everyone. Too many people here knew what your mother wanted," Bob repeated.

Carly sat there. The color drained from her face, and her anger turned to shock. She couldn't believe her mother could be so vindictive. Carly was an only child with no children. They barely had any family, and Carly continued to carry the burden of her parent's choices. It seemed so incredibly unfair.

"Thank you, Bob," Carly said, standing abruptly. "I think I've heard enough for one day." With that, she turned on her heel and exited the law office. She needed some time to think.

Carly walked along the beach, listening to the ocean waves lap against the rocky shoreline. She looked around, admiring the beauty of the ocean. The rocky coast, the blue sky, and the unpredictable waves kept her grounded. Carly tried to change her perspective and think of her mother's gift as a blessing, but the anger and resentment seeped through the cracks with speedy precision.

The inheritance paid for the inn, she already knew how to run it successfully, and she lived in a place where most people dreamed of vacationing. She could never go on vacation on her own because she was trapped here. She could never meet anyone new because no one moved to Block Island unless their family already lived there. Even with the positive thoughts flowing through her mind, the anger and trickery overpowered her psyche.

Carly felt trapped. She had no control of her life and hadn't had control since she returned from Maine. Everything she did was for her family. How could Ruth paralyze her life like this?

Carly didn't necessarily want to sell or leave the island, but her lack of choices made her want to get revenge and teach her parents that she was an individual who could make her own decisions, regardless of how they felt.

Carly made it back to the inn while walking in a daze. Her mind, body, and soul felt numb to the news she received. Her anger subsided, and a dark, empty void traveled from her heart to the pit of her stomach. John, Matt, and Joanie sat at the kitchen table, having the last tuna casserole Mrs. Pickering dropped off before the funeral.

John stood and kissed Carly gently on the lips. He could see the lack of emotion on her face and the paleness of her skin. He poured her a glass of lemonade and invited her to join them at the table. "Are you okay?" he asked semi-privately, away from the others.

Carly nodded, feeling the anger bubble up from her stomach to her throat again. A rock sat on her vocal cords, daring her to stop breathing.

John hugged her, and the floodgates opened wildly. Carly couldn't stop the emotions from pouring out of her onto the kitchen table with all of her friends watching. She cried for the death of her mother, her independence, and her freedom. A bitterness that she didn't even know existed permeated her soul.

Everyone waited uncomfortably for Carly to say the first word. Joanie rubbed her thumb up and down the condensation on her cup. Matt excused himself to go to the bathroom, and John rubbed her back as he pulled her into his chest.

Carly took a deep breath and released a loud sigh. "You guys, she tricked me. I thought that finally, FINALLY," Carly's voice rose in frustration, "I would be able to leave here and follow my heart and my dreams, but I can't. Her will states that the inn goes to me, and any money from selling the inn goes to every small business owner on this island. You guys, I came here to help her! I came here because it was best for the family! I stayed here, sacrificing the life I made—WE MADE," she shot a look at John, "in Maine to help her. I paid my dues to support her, love her, and help her, and THIS is how she pays me? She trapped me into her life with no opportunity to follow my heart, dreams, or desires. I cannot believe she was so selfish! And I never even knew. I should have stood up to her a long time ago. I can't believe I was so stupid!" Carly took a sip of her lemonade and stared out the window. Her thoughts galloped wildly in her brain, and she couldn't keep anything straight. The whole thing seemed unreal.

John grabbed an armful of beers and placed them on the table. "This is for you." He handed one to Carly. "And you," he said, giving one to Joanie. "And us, for being here with you." He handed one to Matt, kept one for himself, and passed around the bottle opener. "Let's have a beer and figure out what this means."

They sat around the table all night, going over the will and precisely what it said. They talked about Joanie losing her job and what her next move should be. They talked about life back in Maine and opportunities there. They talked and talked and talked until the topics went full circle, and an entire twelve-pack of beer was gone.

The stress of the night slowly subsided with each sip of alcohol. They hadn't come to any conclusions. John was returning to Portland, Joanie was returning to Boston, and Carly would still be alone, booking reservations, cooking breakfast, and doing laundry on an island where she knew everyone. Even though life wasn't going to change, she at least had one night where she let all her emotions out on the table. She felt better because nothing was left inside. Her soul felt empty.

Chapter 18

Joanie hustled around the kitchen with a red and white checked apron dangling around her waist. The coffee aroma wafted into the dining room, the bacon sizzled, and the pancakes toasted on the skillet. Joanie piled the food on square plates and placed them on a rolling tea cart. She transferred the drinks to the top shelf and grabbed a handful of napkins.

Some guests she knew, and some were strangers. They sat at the tables with their legs crossed and a newspaper outstretched in front of them. No one looked up when Joanie entered. She looked at their newspapers, and every person was reading the Lifestyle section.

Joanie shook a bell sitting on the tea cart, and all eyes turned to her. She saw Mark, Carly, John, Jackie, Chris, and a group of strangers Joanie didn't recognize. "Hello, everyone! Welcome to breakfast!" Joanie took the food and drink order and quickly dispersed the food. She turned around and found Matt pouring orange juice. He wore a red and black checked chef hat that matched Joanie's apron.

As everyone ate, she saw faint conversations swirling around the room. "She made a change," "She left the newspaper," "She found happiness in the most unexpected place," were random comments that flowed through the air in Times New Roman font. Joanie read them all as they cascaded around her before disappearing into the ceiling.

Joanie tried to talk to Matt about the words she was reading, but no sound came out. She roamed around the room to see if she could read the paper, and in big, bold letters, she read, "From Media to Hospitality: The Willowside Inn Under New Management."

The thoughts and words of all the people eating breakfast swirled until she couldn't see anything but a white fog around her. Everything whipped around her like a tornado, and she screamed in glee. Suddenly, the sound, the words, and the background dropped away, and Joanie was left alone on the beach. She heard a dog barking in the distance and turned to see flashes of light in the sky. Then everything went black.

Joanie opened her eyes instantly. Matt stood over her, holding his camera. "Sorry, you looked so peaceful and beautiful while sleeping. I didn't want to forget you." Joanie sat upright and grabbed his hands.

"Matt. I got it. I know what to do."

Matt looked at her quizzically. "You want to run away together?" he joked.

"No! Yes! Kind of! We—me and you—will take over The Willowside Inn! Carly doesn't have to sell because you are her family. She can live her life, and I will have a job. I won't have to leave you, and Carly won't have to say good-bye to John! For legal purposes, we can manage the property while she still owns it. She can teach us how to do it. It can't be that hard!" Joanie spoke faster and faster, worried that if she took a breath, her idea would vanish.

Matt looked deep into her eyes, trying to ground her. "But I have a job, and I love my job," Matt said.

"No problem! I will run the inn, and you can be my partner. I go to you when I need help brainstorming or help with recipes or when the toilet gets clogged! You will be my sidekick when you are free. Carly will oversee the inn from a distance, and I will do what she asks. Then, when I need help, I will go to you! What do you think?" Joanie jumped out of bed and grabbed her jeans. She quickly brushed her teeth and pulled on her flip-flops.

"Where are you going?" Matt asked, still in bed with the blankets all around him.

"To see Carly! This could work, Matt! This could work!" Joanie ran outside and into the kitchen of the main inn.

Carly and John embraced in the kitchen. His overnight bag was at his feet, and Carly held onto his large frame for three seconds too long. Finally, she disengaged from his arms and kissed him gently and longingly on the lips. Joanie turned her eyes away, feeling uncomfortable witnessing such an intimate moment. She knocked on the door behind her to alert them of her presence.

Carly turned toward Joanie to reveal red, puffy eyes and a sad smile. "Hi Joanie," she said emotionless. Joanie raised her hand in a half-wave and sat down at the kitchen table with a grin as wide as a cantaloupe slice across her face.

"John, are you leaving already?" Joanie asked.

"Yeah, my ferry leaves at 10:15. I could only take off a few days of work. This is our busiest fishing time, so I can't leave my lobster boat for much longer. I'm going to get back tonight and start work again tomorrow."

Joanie looked at her watch. It was 8:45, and she knew that they could give her at least ten minutes of their time before he had to go. Joanie felt awful for interrupting their private time but knew that if she didn't share her thoughts now, the excitement would pass and who knows where they would all end up.

"Have a safe trip back. It was nice meeting you. I can see that you make Carly happy and that makes me happy. She's my only friend here, and she deserves to be happy."

"Thanks. It was great meeting you too," John said. Silence filled the space between them, and Joanie could tell that they wanted her to leave.

"Uh, okay. I promise I won't be here long, but I have to tell you! I have a perfect idea! It is perfect for you and me!" Joanie said, gesturing to Carly. "And you need to stay," she turned to John, "because it involves you too!"

Carly leaned against the kitchen counter, sipping her steaming mug of coffee. "What is it?"

"Okay, listen. You go with John, and I stay here with Matt. We'll take care of this place!" Joanie spilled the news like an overflowing bucket.

"But I can't do that. I have to stay here. It's in the will," Carly said sadly.

"No, it's not!" Joanie exclaimed. "The will says you can't sell, but it doesn't say anything about you staying on this island. It says it has to stay in the family. Matt is your family! If you feel guilty about leaving the inn to a stranger, don't! Matt agreed to help me anytime I need help!"

John rubbed Carly's back, and Carly stood up straight.

"But…" she began, "You don't know anything about running a bed and breakfast."

"Oh please!" Joanie replied. "How hard can it be? Plus, we have a few more weeks until Labor Day, which is when things considerably slow down. So, you can teach me for the last of the summer season, and then head off to Maine or wherever you want to go in the fall, and I will slowly work my way into running this place!"

Carly stared at her blankly, processing the idea.

"Plus," Joanie continued, "we are just a phone call away! If I truly run into a problem, I will call you! Don't you see? This is your ticket to living the life you want and the life you deserve! You guys deserve to be together. Your story never ended, you guys. It paused because life happened. It never ended!"

Carly started crying quietly into her hands, leaning on the granite countertop. Matt rubbed her back and pulled her into a hug. "Carly," John whispered, "I have to go."

Carly nodded, told Joanie she needed some time to think, and they exited the house to say one last goodbye. Joanie watched them walk down the deserted, narrow road toward town until they disappeared into the horizon.

She felt defeated, but at least she poured her idea out like it was her final lifeline. If this didn't work, she didn't know what she was going to do. Joanie walked back to the carriage house to find Matt drinking a cup of coffee at the kitchen table. Joanie joined him and recounted her conversation with John and Carly. They decided the best thing they could do was enjoy their time because neither knew how much longer they had together.

Epilogue

"Welcome to breakfast at The Willowside Inn!" Joanie bellowed as she entered the nearly empty dining room. Her sister, Jackie, smiled at her. Jackie held up her coffee mug and clinked mugs with Chris.

"Cheers!" she said.

Joanie walked over to their table with two plates full of pancakes, bacon, sausage, home fries, and scrambled eggs. Joanie waited until they took their first bite.

"Yum!" Jackie exclaimed. "I had no idea you could cook!"

"I couldn't, and I was terrible at it when I first started, but Carly was patient with me and taught me well! You have no idea how many breakfast dinners Matt and I have had to perfect my technique. This is pretty much all I can cook without burning down the kitchen. Chris, what do you think?" Joanie asked, indirectly asking for compliments.

"So good!" Chris replied. "Ever since I was a kid, I wondered what it was like to stay here. Carly and I were in different classes, so we didn't really hang out, but every time my parents had friends or family over, she always recommended this place."

"I am so happy you guys came! I know the weather is kind of iffy, so I appreciate you making an effort to travel." Joanie looked out the window and took in the collision of gray, depressing skies and glowing bright snow. A dusting of snow covered the road in front of the inn. It was breathtaking.

"Of course," Jackie answered. "How was Mom and Dad's visit?" Joanie's parents traveled to New England for Christmas and came to the island for two nights.

"They were shocked that my life had turned in the direction it had. I was so nervous about having them here because they have never been proud or excited about my life choices, but I think they had a good time. There were no kinks, and I made Carly and John come back for that weekend, just in case I screwed something up and Mom and Dad had more reason to believe that my life was going down the toilet."

Jackie smiled. "I stopped caring a long time ago about what they thought of me. They weren't excited when Chris and I moved in together because we weren't married. They pretended to be happy, but they were appalled when I bought an over-the-top expensive car. I was working retail, making minimum wage. They hated that I moved halfway across the country to get away from them. It's okay, Joanie. We all make our choices, and as long as you are okay with them, then who cares what they think?"

Joanie always admired her sister's confidence, even when the poise was fake. "Yeah, I guess we are all just faking life, right? We're trying to get through the days the best we can. You're right, though. I am happy. I am happy that I got myself out of Boston, away from that soul-sucking job, and happy that I pushed myself out of my comfort zone. I do love it here. Even though it's been slow because of the weather and the time of year, I feel like I'm making a difference, even if that difference is just making people's visits and vacations a little more enjoyable."

"Tell me about Matt," Chris said. "I had no idea you were dating him until Jackie showed me a picture of you two at Thanksgiving. He was older than me, so I didn't know him, but I remember seeing him at Carly's when we were kids. He seemed like a good guy."

"Yes! He is such a good guy. He is patient with me, lets me be me, and makes me laugh. He has been so helpful with this transition. We are serious, but we don't talk about it. I feel like labels complicate things. He still lives at his house, and I live here, but he comes over at least three times a week. Sometimes he comes over as my manager." Joanie air quoted the word manager. "And sometimes he comes over as my boyfriend." Joanie air quoted that word too.

"Do you think he could be the one?" Jackie asked

"Honestly, I don't know. I'm going to be forty in a few months. I have given up on marriage, but if he and I can enjoy each other's company, I'm happy. I don't need a husband. So far, he has come through for me in every crisis. He's amazing."

"Where is he now?" Chris asked.

"He worked the overnight shift. I think he'll be here later, after he naps and showers. Usually, he comes in around one or so. You'll see him before you leave tomorrow. Don't worry!" Joanie said.

That morning, the three of them watched the snowfall, drank hot chocolate, and watched movies. Matt came over at two, just as Joanie predicted. They kissed each other when he walked in, and Matt gave Chris a bro hug, even though they didn't know each other. They cooked dinner together, and the four of them spent the night playing cards.

Joanie felt terrific and couldn't believe how her life had changed in less than a year. Even if she and Matt didn't work out, she knew that their time together was for the best. She no longer felt stuck in a life that felt out of control or paralyzed in a job she hated. She realized with certainty that she finally felt alive. Even if this job didn't work out, she knew that her willingness to change helped Carly chase her dreams. Joanie smiled to herself, excited for her future.

* * *

"John! Can you grab me a beer?" Carly yelled into the kitchen. She curled up on the couch under a blanket, binging the latest drama. They had been inside for twenty-four hours because a Nor'easter had hit and dumped twelve inches of snow. Carly missed these days where she could sit and do nothing. She didn't have to do laundry for other people, cook other people's food, or spend half the day traveling to see her mother. Sometimes stopping was the best thing she could do to take care of herself.

Moving in with John was one of the scariest things she had done. She wanted to leave the island, but the idea of actually going terrified her. She wasn't happy running the inn, but it was comfortable and predictable, and she was good at it. Leaving meant starting over in a new city with no job with a man she hadn't interacted with for almost a decade. Carly at age thirty was very different from Carly at age forty. A lot of life had happened for both of them, and there was no guarantee that they would mesh the way they remembered.

Carly's mother left her some money, which gave her the courage to pack up and leave. Even if it was the worst decision and her entire life crumbled in this foreign place, she could still return home. She still had a fully paid home and could return to the life she lived without John.

Carly hung around the inn until October, which was enough time to feel confident that Joanie and Matt could manage. John came back to Maine and worked until Lobster season was over without Carly. They decided that it was best to find an apartment together instead of Carly moving into John's place. It allowed them both to leave their past behind and create a new life together. Plus, John was a bachelor, so he lived in a studio the size of Carly's bedroom at home.

They found a cute two-bedroom apartment outside of downtown, but within walking distance to all the shops and restaurants. Carly didn't want to overpower the planning, so they compromised and filled their apartment with just the basics. Carly found a job waitressing at her old restaurant, which helped her transition into her old life. The old friends she had had all moved on, but at least she was familiar with the menu.

John's work ended when Carly moved back, which allowed them time to reconnect. In addition, he picked up a side job driving for Uber and worked when Carly worked so that they could see each other as often as possible.

John sat down next to Carly and gave her a local craft beer bottle. They watched seven hours of TV together, curled up under the blanket on the couch.

Carly knew that life wouldn't be like this forever but did her best to be brave and enjoy every single moment. Life could change as quickly as the weather, and Carly knew that every weather phenomenon had beauty if you looked hard enough. At that moment, she felt joy in recognizing the beauty of her situation.

***

What happens when Carly discovers a secret that destroys everything she believed about her past? Find out here!

Excerpt From *HOPE HANNA MURPHY*
Story Two of the Block Island Saga

She had played the scenario out in her mind at least a million times. The outcome was always the same, but her approach was different. She didn't know what would be best. Accusations of abandonment? Sympathy for the difficult choices life forced her to make? Immediate acceptance despite the pain and confusion? She wasn't sure which approach would result in the best outcome.

She was angry. Her entire life was a lie, yet her parents led her to believe that nothing was out of place. They all had a role to play and played it flawlessly. She thought that they wanted what was best for her when they were only looking out for themselves.

People she didn't know filed into the upholstered seats around the floral trellis. This wasn't her day, but it was undoubtedly about her. She painted a smile on her face, anxiously scanning the eyes staring back at her. Some looked familiar, and some looked unknown. The face she searched for was both comforting and strange.

Her eyes scanned the crowd haphazardly until she settled on a man and older woman across the aisle. She was looking in a mirror. Same petite frame, same round eyes, and same crooked smile stared back at her. It was her, just older. Her body filled with heat, and her feet started to sweat. She pulled off her pumps and placed her feet in the cool, dry grass. The blades rubbed her feet and sent shivers up her spine to the base of her neck.

The room began to spin. She couldn't take her eyes off of her. She wondered if she knew she was there or if she thought she would be alone, unnoticed. The bride and groom walked down the aisle, declaring their love. All the buried emotions emerged as a twister, preparing to touch down and wreak havoc on the lives of many.

She gulped down the rest of the wine she sneaked to her seat, hiding the glass behind the chair's leg. Liquid courage traversed throughout her body, and her bravery overpowered her fear. She knew it was risky because the truth could come out, but it needed to be said. She rehearsed it over and over in her mind. Suddenly, she was standing face to face with the ghost of her past, despite her ignorance and naivety.

She screamed out the words in her head, but her mouth remained silent. *Mom, why did you leave me?*

Get your copy today!

About the Author

E.D. Hackett lives with her husband, two children, and three fur babies in Massachusetts. She always enjoyed writing short stories and journaling when she was a child. She majored in Journalism for a hot second in college and eventually graduated with a Master's degree in Speech-language pathology. E.D. Hackett is an SLP by day and a writer by night.

For most of her adult years, her writing was placed on the back burner due to the chaos of full-time parenting and full-time work. With a little encouragement, she decided to write a novel, write it well, and write it scared. Hope Hanna Murphy is her third novel.

She hopes to convey themes that are relatable to all women and hopes they are enjoyed by all readers. She can be found on Facebook, Instagram, and Goodreads, as well as her website www.edhackettwrites.com

You can connect with me on:

🌐 https://www.edhackettwrites.com

📘 https://www.facebook.com/edhackettwrites

🔗 https://linktr.ee/Edhackett

Subscribe to my newsletter:

✉ https://www.edhackettwrites.com/contact

Also by E.D. Hackett

E.D. Hackett writes Women's Fiction novels that address self-discovery, friendship, family, and finding happiness.

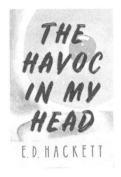

The Havoc in My Head

Ashley Martin has the perfect life and her need to control was the reason why her life was unfolding just as she expected. When people looked at her, they wanted to be in her shoes, with the supportive husband, well-behaved kids, beautiful home, and highly respected job. Unexpectedly, a terrifying medical diagnosis shatters Ashley's perfect life and she wonders how she will pick up the broken pieces.

After a plethora of symptoms led Ashley to the ER, her life is turned upside down in an instant, and her definition of happiness and success crumbles between her fingers. As Ashley stumbles through the medical maze she is forced to travel, she struggles with isolation and loneliness as her identity is slowly stripped away. Ashley simmers with her thoughts, realizing that her marriage is broken, she doesn't know her children, and she was replaceable and disposable at work.

Can Ashley accept the path that is before her and find the strength to battle and survive while learning how to redefine what a happy, successful life means?

Hope Hanna Murphy

Sometimes the life you created and loved isn't your life at all.

She sacrificed too much for them. When her real ancestry shatters her world, will she ever reclaim happiness?

Carly Davis was sure getting away from the island would help. Elated after finally freeing herself from running her late family's inn, her fresh start in Maine fizzles in the aftermath of a failed relationship. And her luck sours further still when an innocent DNA test reveals at least one of her parents had been deceiving her for decades.

Furious she gave up the best years of her life to support people she wasn't even related to, the distraught woman returns home to seek answers about her actual origins. But with her dear friend's sister marrying a guy who is suddenly Carly's cousin, the angry adoptee fears the truth could leave her more alone than ever...

Will she find the joy she so desperately craves, or will her true heritage only bring new sorrow?

Hope Hanna Murphy is the enchanting second book in The Block Island Saga women's fiction series. If you like optimistic stories, conflicted characters, and the strength of community, then you'll love E.D. Hackett's tale of courage.

Reinventing Amara Leventis
She wants everyone to think she's got it together. So where did it all fall apart?

Providence, RI. Amara Leventis craves validation. So when her best friend and roomie gets engaged, the twenty-five-year-old single girl fears she's losing her soulmate… and her apartment forever. Reeling from the sense of abandonment, Amara turns an interview for a work promotion into a shocking pink slip.

Humiliated and effectively homeless, the frazzled woman begrudgingly returns to rural Connecticut and her parents' Greek bakery. But when a fight gets her bounced from the wedding party and she discovers her dad's troubling secrets, Amara wonders if life will always be sour instead of sweet.

Will she ever find the right recipe for happiness?

Reinventing Amara Leventis is a richly drawn women's fiction novel. If you like relatable characters, family dramas, and laugh-out-loud moments, then you'll adore E.D. Hackett's entertaining read.

Made in the USA
Monee, IL
31 July 2022

10652579R00085